Street Sense,
Jessica Mused.

Odd that the term should bring James Sladerman into her mind. Yet even in that quick exchange at the foot of the stairs, she'd felt something in him. It told her that he was a man who would know how to handle himself—in business, maybe. In an alley, definitely. With a half laugh, she stuck her hands in her pockets. Now why should she think of that?

It had been his eyes. There had been something . . . hard in his eyes. Yet she hadn't been frightened, but drawn. He'd made her feel safe, Jessica realized.

And that brought up another question. How would James Sladerman be at handling a woman?

Dear Reader:

There is an electricity between two people in love that makes everything they do magic, larger than life. This is what we bring you in SILHOUETTE INTIMATE MOMENTS.

SILHOUETTE INTIMATE MOMENTS are longer, more sensuous romance novels filled with adventure, suspense, glamor or melodrama. These books have an element no one else has tapped: excitement.

We are proud to present the very best romance has to offer from the very best romance writers. In the coming months look for some of your favorite authors such as Elizabeth Lowell, Nora Roberts, Erin St. Claire and Brooke Hastings.

SILHOUETTE INTIMATE MOMENTS are for the woman who wants more than she has ever had before. These books are for you.

Karen Solem
Editor-in-Chief
Silhouette Books

A Matter Of Choice

Nora Roberts

Silhouette Intimate Moments

Published by Silhouette Books New York

America's Publisher of Contemporary Romance

To Karen Solem,
for the support and the friendship

SILHOUETTE BOOKS, a Division of Simon & Schuster, Inc.
1230 Avenue of the Americas, New York, N.Y. 10020

ISBN: 0-671-50295-6

First Silhouette Books printing May, 1984

10 9 8 7 6 5 4 3 2 1

Books by Nora Roberts

Silhouette Romance

Irish Thoroughbred #81
Blithe Images #127
Song of the West #143
Search for Love #163
Island of Flowers #180
From This Day #199
Her Mother's Keeper #215
Untamed #252
Storm Warning #274
Sullivan's Woman #280

Silhouette Special Edition

The Heart's Victory #59
Reflections #100
Dance of Dreams #116
First Impressions #162

Silhouette Intimate Moments

Once More with Feeling #2
Tonight and Always #12
This Magic Moment #25
Endings and Beginnings #33
A Matter of Choice #49

Pocket Books

Promise Me Tomorrow

Prologue

JAMES SLADERMAN FROWNED AT THE TOE OF HIS SHOE. He'd been frowning since the summons from Commissioner Dodson had reached him in the squad room that morning. After blowing out a long stream of smoke, Slade crushed out the cigarette in the mosaic ashtray to his left. He barely shifted his body. Slade knew how to wait.

Only the night before he had waited for more than five hours in a dark, chilly car in a neighborhood where it paid to watch your back as well as your wallet. It had been a tedious, fruitless five hours, as the stakeout had produced nothing. But then, Slade knew from long experience that police work consisted of hours of endless legwork, impossible boredom, and paperwork, punctuated by moments of stark violence. Still he preferred the five-hour wait to the twenty minutes he had spent in the commissioner's carpeted, beige-walled outer office. It smelled of lemony polish and now, his own Virginia tobacco. The keys of a typewriter clattered with monotonous efficiency as the commissioner's secretary transcribed.

What the hell does he want? Slade wondered again. Throughout his career Slade had studiously avoided the politics of police work because of an inherent dislike of bureaucracy. In his climb from cadet to detective sergeant, there had been little opportunity for his path to cross Dodson's.

Slade had had brief personal contact with Dodson at his father's funeral. Captain Thomas C. Sladerman had been buried with all the glory and honor that comes from serving on the force for twenty-eight years. And dying in the line of duty. Mulling over it, Slade recalled that the commissioner had been sympathetic to the widow and the young daughter. He'd said the right things to the son. Perhaps on some level he had been personally grieved. Early in their careers Dodson and Sladerman had been partners. They had still been young men when their paths had separated —one finding a niche in politics and administration, the other craving the action of the streets.

On only one other occasion had Slade had one-to-one contact with Dodson. Then Slade had been in the hospital, recovering from a gunshot wound. The visit of the commissioner of police to a mere detective had resulted in talk and speculation that had embarrassed Slade as much as annoyed him.

Now, he realized, it would be all over the station house that the old man had called him in. His frown became a scowl. For a moment he wondered if he had committed some breach in procedure, then became furious with himself for behaving like a kid hauled before the school principal.

The hell with it, he decided, forcing himself to relax. The chair was soft—too soft, and too short. To compensate, Slade curved his spine into the back and stretched out his long legs. His eyes half closed. When the interview was over, he had the stakeout to look forward to again. If it went down tonight, he'd have a few evenings free to spend at the typewriter. With any luck—and a solid month without interruptions—he could finish the novel. Blocking out his surroundings, he mentally reviewed the chapter he was working on.

"Sergeant Sladerman?"

Annoyed by the distraction, Slade lifted his eyes. Slowly his expression cleared. He realized he'd wasted his time staring at the floor when the commissioner's secretary provided a far more appealing view. His smile was at once appraising and charming.

"The commissioner will see you now." The secretary answered the smile, wishing he'd looked at her like that before, rather than sitting in sullen silence. He had a face any female would respond to—a bit narrow, angular, with dark coloring that came from Italian ancestors on his mother's side. The mouth had been hard in repose, but now, curved, it showed both promise and passion. Black hair and gray eyes were an irresistible combination, especially, she thought, when the hair was thick and a bit unruly and the eyes were smoky and mysterious. He was an interesting prospect, she thought as she watched Slade unfold his long, rangy frame from the chair.

As he followed her to the oak door he noted that

the ring finger of her left hand was bare. Idly, he considered getting her phone number on the way out. The thought slipped to the back of his mind as she ushered him into the commissioner's office.

There was a Perillo lithograph on the right wall—a lone cowboy astride a paint pony. The left wall was crowded with framed photos, commendations, diplomas. If Slade found it an odd combination, he gave no sign. The desk, with its back to the window, was dark oak. On it were papers in tidy stacks, a gold pen and pencil set, and a triple picture frame. Seated behind them was Dodson, a dark, tidy little man who had always reminded Slade more of a parish priest than New York's commissioner of police. His eyes were a calm, pale blue, his cheeks healthily ruddy. Thin wisps of white wove through his hair. All in all, Dodson was the picture of avuncular gentleness. But the lines in his face hadn't been etched by good humor.

"Sergeant Sladerman." Dodson motioned Slade to a chair with a gesture and a smile. Built like his father, he thought briefly as he watched Slade take his seat. "Did I keep you waiting?"

"A bit."

Like his father, Dodson thought again, managing not to smile. Except that there'd been talk that the son's real interest lay in writing, not in police work. Tom had always brushed that aside, Dodson remembered. *My boy's a cop, just like his old man. A damn good cop.* At the moment Dodson was banking on it.

"How's the family?" he asked casually while keeping those deceptive blue eyes direct.

"Fine. Thank you, sir."

"Janice is enjoying college?" He offered Slade a cigar. When it was refused, Dodson lit one for himself. Slade waited until the smoke stung the air before answering. Just how, he wondered, did Dodson know his sister was in college?

"Yes, she likes it."

"How's the writing?"

He had to call on all of his training not to reveal surprise at the question. His eyes remained as clear and steady as his voice. "Struggling."

No time for small talk, Dodson thought, tapping off cigar ash. The boy's already itching to be gone. But being commissioner gave him an advantage. He took another slow drag of the cigar, watching the smoke curl lazily toward the ceiling. "I read that short story of yours in *Mirror*," Dodson went on. "It was very good."

"Thank you." What the hell's the point? Slade wondered impatiently.

"No luck with the novel?"

Briefly, almost imperceptively, Slade's eyes narrowed. "Not yet."

Sitting back, Dodson chewed on his cigar as he studied the man across from him. Had the look of his father, too, he mused. Slade had the same narrow face that was both intelligent and tough. He wondered if the son could smile with the same disarming charm as the father. Yet the eyes were like his mother's— dark gray and thoughtful, skilled at keeping emotions hidden. Then there was his record, Dodson mused. He might not be the flashy cop his father had been, but he was thorough. And, thank God, less impulsive. After his years on the force, the last three in homicide, Slade could be considered seasoned. If an undercover cop wasn't seasoned by thirty-two, he was dead. Slade had a reputation for being cool, perhaps a shade too cool, but his arrests were clean. Dodson didn't need a man who looked for trouble, but one who knew what to do once he found it.

"Slade . . ." He allowed a small smile to escape. "That's what you're called, isn't it?"

"Yes, sir." The familiarity made him uncomfortable; the smile made him suspicious.

"I'm sure you've heard of Justice Lawrence Winslow."

Curiosity came first, then a quick search through his mental file. "Presided over the New York Appellate Court before he was elected chief justice of the Connecticut Supreme Court about fifteen years ago. Died of a heart attack four, maybe five years ago."

Facts and figures, Dodson mused. The boy didn't waste words. "He was also a damn fine lawyer, a judge who understood the full meaning of justice. A good man. His wife remarried two years ago and lives in southern France."

So what? Slade thought with fresh impatience as Dodson gazed broodingly over his shoulder.

"I'm godfather to his daughter, Jessica." The same question zipped through Slade's mind as Dodson focused on him again. "She lives in the family home near Westport. Beautiful place—a stone's throw from the beach. It's quiet, peaceful." He drummed his fingers against the desk. "I imagine a writer would find it very appealing."

There was an uncomfortable premonition which Slade pushed aside. "Possibly." Was the old man matchmaking? Slade almost laughed out loud. No, that was too ridiculous.

"Over the last nine months there has been a rash of thefts throughout Europe."

The abrupt change of subject startled Slade so much that the surprise showed clearly on his face. Quickly he controlled it and lifted a brow, saying nothing.

"Important thefts," Dodson continued. "Mainly from museums—gems, coins, stamps. France, England, Spain, and Italy have all been hit. The investigation has led the respective authorities to believe the stolen articles have been smuggled into the States."

"Smuggling's federal," Slade said briefly. And, he thought silently, has nothing to do with a homicide detective—or some justice's spoiled daughter. Another uncomfortable thought came to him which he ignored.

"Smuggling's federal," Dodson repeated, a bit too amiably for Slade's taste. He placed the tips of his neat fingers together, watching the younger man over them. "I have a few connections in the Bureau. Because of this case's . . . delicate nature, I've been consulted." He paused a beat, long enough for Slade to comment if he chose to, then went on. "Some substantial leads in the investigation point to a small, well-respected antique shop. The Bureau knows there's an operator. From the information I have, they've narrowed down the possibilities for dump sites, and this shop is one of the . . . chosen few," he decided dryly. "It's believed someone on the inside is on the take." Pausing, he adjusted the picture frame on his desk. "They want to put an operative on it, inside, so that the head of the organization won't slip away from them this time. He's clever," Dodson mused, half to himself.

Again Dodson gave Slade a moment to question or comment, and again he went on as the other man remained silent. "Allegedly, the goods are hidden—cleverly hidden—in an antique, then exported to this shop, retrieved, and ultimately disposed of."

"It seems the Feds have things under control." Barely masking his impatience, Slade reached for a cigarette.

"There're one or two complications." Dodson waited for the hiss and flare of the match. "There's no concrete evidence, nor is the identity of the head of the organization known. A handful of accomplices, yes, but we want him . . . or her," he added softly.

The tone had Slade's eyes sharpening. Don't get interested, he warned himself. It has nothing to do with you. Swallowing the questions that had popped into his head, he drew on his cigarette and waited.

"There's also a more delicate problem." For the first time since Slade had walked into the room, he noticed Dodson's nerves. The commissioner picked up his gold pen, ran it through his fingers, then stuck it back in its slot. "The antique shop alleged to be involved is owned and operated by my goddaughter."

Dark brows lifted, but the eyes beneath them betrayed nothing. "Justice Winslow's daughter."

"It's generally believed that Jessica knows nothing of the illegal use of her shop—if indeed there is illegal use." Dodson reached for the pen again, this time holding it lengthwise between both hands. "I know she's completely innocent. Not only because she's my goddaughter," he went on, anticipating Slade's thoughts, "but because I know her. She's every bit as honest as her father was. Jessica cherishes Larry's memory. And," he added, carefully setting down the pen, "she hardly needs the money."

"Hardly," Slade muttered, picturing a spoiled heiress with too much time and money on her hands. Smuggling for kicks, he mused. A change of pace from shopping and parties and jet-setting.

"The Bureau's closing in," Dodson stated. "The next few weeks could bring the whole mess down around her ears. It might be dangerous for her." Slade controlled the snort of derision. "Even the shield of ignorance isn't going to protect her once things come to a head if her shop's involved. I've tried to convince her to come to New York for a visit, but . . ." His voice trailed off. Amused exasperation moved over his face. "Jessica's stubborn. Claims she's too busy. She tells me I should come visit her." With a shake of his head, Dodson let out what passed for a sigh. "I considered it, but my presence at this point could jeopardize the investigation. However, I feel Jessica needs protection. Discreet protection. Someone trained to deal with the situation, who can stay close to her without causing speculation." A smile touched his eyes. "Someone who could assist the investigation from the inside."

Slade frowned. He liked the conversation less and less. Taking his time, he stubbed out his cigarette. "And how do you expect me to do that?"

Dodson smiled fully. He liked the irritation in Slade's voice as much as the directness. "Jessica will do what I want—to a point." Leaning back in the overstuffed leather chair, he relaxed again. "She's been complaining lately about the mess her library's in, about not having enough time to sort through and catalog. I'm going to call her, tell her I'm sending the son of an old friend of mine and her father's. That's true, by the way," he added. "Tom and Larry knew each other some years back. Your cover's simple enough. You're a writer who needs a quiet refuge for a few weeks, and in turn, you'll sort out her library."

Slade's eyes had darkened during Dodson's casual rundown. "Jurisdiction—" he began.

"Some paperwork," Dodson interrupted easily. "It can be taken care of. After all, it's the boys from the Bureau who'll make the collar when it's time."

"I'm supposed to play librarian and baby sitter." Slade gave a snort of disgust. "Look, Commissioner, I'm that close to wrapping up the Bitronelli murder." He brought his thumb and forefinger together. "If—"

"You'd better be," Dodson interrupted again, but with a hint of steel in his voice. "The press is having a great time making the NYPD look like fools on that one. And if you're so close," he added before Slade could toss back a furious retort, "you should be able to leave for Connecticut in a couple of days. The Bureau is interested in having a cop on the inside. A cop who knows how to keep his eyes and ears open. They've checked you out and agree with my choice."

"Terrific," Slade muttered. Standing, he prowled the room. "I'm homicide, not robbery."

"You're a cop," Dodson said shortly.

"Yeah." Baby-sitting for some snobby little heiress, Slade thought darkly, who was either smuggling for thrills or too dizzy to see what was going on under her nose. "Terrific," he muttered again.

Once Janice was out of college, he thought, he could quit the force and concentrate on his writing. He was tired of it. Tired of the misery he came in contact with almost every day of his life. Tired of the dirt, the futility, tired of the nasty little pieces of humanity his job forced him to deal with. And tired too of seeing the look of relief in his mother's eyes each time he came home. With a sigh, he resigned himself. Maybe a couple of weeks in Connecticut would be a nice change. A change anyway.

"When?" he demanded as he turned back to face Dodson.

"Day after tomorrow," Dodson said smoothly. "I'll give you a complete briefing, then I'll call Jessica and tell her to expect you."

With a shrug, Slade went back to his chair to listen.

Chapter 1

FALL TOUCHED THE TREES AND STUNG THE AIR. AGAINST a hard blue sky, the colors were vibrant, passionate. The ribbon of road cut through the hills and wound eastward toward the Atlantic. Whipping through the open car windows, the wind was chilled and fragrant. Slade wondered how long it had been since he had smelled that kind of freshness. No city smells of sweat and exhaust. When his book was accepted, perhaps he could move his mother and Janice out of the city—a home in the country maybe, or near the shore. It was always *when* or *as soon as*. He couldn't afford to think *if*.

Another year on the force—another year of scraping up tuition money—and then. . . . Shaking his head, Slade turned up the radio. It wasn't any good thinking of next year. He wasn't in Connecticut to appreciate the scenery. It was just another job—and one he resented.

Jessica Winslow, he mused, age twenty-seven. The only child of Justice Lawrence Winslow and Lorraine Nordan Winslow. Graduate of Radcliffe, senior class president. She'd probably been head cheerleader, too, he thought with a sneer. All button-downed and pony-tailed. Ralph Lauren sweaters and Gucci loafers.

Struggling to be open minded, he continued his catalog. Opened the House of Winslow four years ago. Up until two years ago she did the majority of buying herself. Good excuse to play around in Europe, he thought as he punched in the car lighter.

Michael Adams, Jessica Winslow's assistant and current buyer. Thirty-two, Yale graduate. Figures, Slade reflected, exhaling smoke that rushed out of the open window. Son of Robert and Marion Adams, another prominent Connecticut family. No firm evidence, but someone Slade was instructed to keep his eye on. He leaned his elbow on the window as he considered. As chief buyer, Adams would be in a perfect position to handle the operation from overseas.

David Ryce, shop assistant for eighteen months. Twenty-three. Son of Elizabeth Ryce, the Winslow housekeeper. Dodson had said he was often trusted with running the shop alone. That would give him the opportunity to handle the local operation.

Systematically, Slade ran through the list of the Winslow staff. Gardener, cook, housekeeper, daily maid. Good God, he thought in disgust. All that for one person. She probably wouldn't know how to boil an egg if her life depended on it.

The gates to the Winslow estate stood open, with room enough for two cars to pass easily. Slade turned into the long, macadam drive, lined with bushy, bloomless azaleas. There was a burst of birdsong, then silence. He drove nearly a quarter of a mile before pulling up in front of the house.

It was large but, he had to admit, not oppressively so. The brick was old, mellowed by sun and sea air. Smoke rose from one of the chimneys on the hipped roof. The gray shutters weren't just decorative, he noted, but could be used for practical purposes if a storm rose up off the Sound. He smelled the chrysanthemums before he saw them.

The blossoms were huge, growing near the base of the house. They were rust, gold, and copper, complimenting the violent red of bushes. It charmed him, as did the lazy odor of woodsmoke. This wasn't indolence but peace. He'd had too little of that. Shaking off the mood, Slade walked up the steps to the front door. He lifted a fist and knocked, hard. He hated doorbells.

In less than a minute the door opened. He had to look down, quite a distance down, to see a tiny, middle-aged woman with a pleasantly ugly face and gray-streaked hair. He caught a whiff of a pine-scented cleaner that reminded him of his mother's kitchen.

"May I help you?" The accent was broad New England.

"I'm James Sladerman. Miss Winslow's expecting me."

The woman scrutinized him with cautious black eyes. "You'd be the writer," she stated, obviously not overly impressed. Stepping back, she allowed him to enter.

As the door closed behind him, Slade glanced around the hall. The floor was uncarpeted, a gleaming blond oak that showed some wear under the careful polishing. A few paintings hung on the ivory-toned wallpaper. A pale green glass bowl sat on a high round table and overflowed with fall flowers. There were no overt displays of wealth, but wealth was there. He'd seen a print of the painting to his right in an art book. The blue scarf that hung negligently over the railing of the steps was silk.

Slade started to turn back to the housekeeper when a clatter at the top of the steps distracted him.

She came barrelling down the curved staircase in a flurry of swirling blond hair and flying skirts. The hammer of heels on wood disrupted the quiet of the house. Slade had a quick impression of speed, motion, and energy.

"Betsy, you make David stay in bed until that fever's broken. Don't you dare let him get up. Damn, damn, damn, I'm going to be late! Where are my keys?"

Three inches away from Slade, she came to a screeching halt, almost overbalancing. Automatically he reached for her arm to steady her. Breathless, she brought her eyes from his shirt front to stare at him.

It was an exquisite face—fair skinned, oval, delicate, with just a hint of cheekbone that added a rather primitive strength. Indian? Viking? he wondered. Celtic? Her eyes were large, the color of aged whiskey, set below brows that were lowered in curiosity. The faintest line appeared between them. A stubborn line, Slade reflected. His sister had one. She was small, he noted. The top of her head barely skimmed his shoulder. Her scent was reminiscent of fall— something musky—blossoms and smoke. The arm beneath his hand was slender under a thin wool blazer. He felt the stir inside him—man for woman— and hastily dropped his hand.

"This is Mr. Sladerman," Betsy announced. "That writer."

"Oh yes." The smile cleared away the faint line between her brows. "Uncle Charlie told me you were coming."

It took Slade a moment to connect Uncle Charlie with Dodson. Not knowing if he was smothering an oath or a laugh, he accepted her extended hand. "Charlie told me you could use some help, Miss Winslow."

"Help." She rolled her eyes and cleared her throat. "Yes, you could call it that. The library. . . . Look, I'm sorry to rush off the minute you get here, but my assistant's ill and my buyer's in France." Tilting her wrist, she grimaced at her watch. "I have a client coming to the shop ten minutes ago."

"Don't worry about it." If this frazzled lady can run a business, I'll volunteer to walk a beat, he decided, but gave her an easy smile. "It'll give me a chance to get settled in."

"Fine. I'll see you at dinner then." Glancing around, she muttered again about keys.

"In your hand," Slade told her.

"Stupid." With a sigh, Jessica uncurled her fingers and stared at the keys in her palm. "The more I have to rush, the worse it gets." Lifting amused eyes to his, she brushed her hair from her shoulders. "Please don't bother with the library today. It may shock you so much that you'll run away before I can smooth things over. Betsy . . ." As she dashed for the door Jessica looked over her shoulder. "Tell David he's fired if he gets out of bed. 'Bye."

The door slammed behind her. Betsy clucked her tongue.

Ten minutes later Slade inspected his suite of rooms. They were nearly as large as the apartment he had grown up in. There was a faded carpet on the bedroom floor that he recognized was not *old* but *antique*. In a small, black marble fireplace, wood was neatly laid for burning. Crossing to the sitting room, he saw a sturdy desk topped with a vase of the chrysanthemums, a brass paperweight, and a feather quill. Without hesitation, he cleared it off to make room for his typewriter.

If he had his way, his writing would be more than a cover. When he wasn't baby-sitting, he'd get some work done. Of course, there was the library to fool with. On an exasperated sigh, Slade turned his back on his typewriter and went back downstairs. He roamed, filing the position and layout of rooms in the cop's part of his mind, their descriptions in the writer's.

In his tour of the first floor, Slade could find no fault with Jessica's taste. It was only the nouveau riche who went in for ostentation. The Winslow woman preferred muted colors and clean lines. In her clothes, too, he mused, remembering how she had looked in the dun-colored blazer and skirt. Still, the blouse she'd worn had been a deep, almost violent green. That just might indicate something else.

Slade stopped to run his fingers over the surface of a rosewood piano. Compared to this, he mused, the battered upright his mother treasured was so much kindling. With a shrug, he wandered to the next door.

The library. He caught the scent of old leather and dust as he looked on the largest private collection of books he'd ever seen. For the first time since he had walked into Dodson's office, Slade felt a stir of pleasure. A quick study told him that the books were well read as well as carelessly filed. He crossed the room and mounted the two stairs to the second level. Not filed at all, he corrected, but simply jumbled. He ran a long finger along a row of volumes. Robert Burns tilted onto a copy of Kurt Vonnegut.

A big job, he concluded. One he might have enjoyed if it had been his only purpose. He took one long look around before absently pulling out a book. There was nothing he could do about Jessica Winslow at the moment, he thought as he settled down to read.

Jessica swerved into the parking area beside her shop, relieved to see it empty. She was late, but her client was later. Or, she thought with a frown, he'd grown tired of waiting and left. With a half-hearted oath, she hurried to unlock the front door. Quickly she went from window to window, letting the shades snap up. Without slackening pace, she headed for the back room, tossed her purse aside, then filled a small kettle with water. She gave the struggling ivy in the rear window a quick douse before setting the kettle on the stove. Halfway out of the room, she went back to turn the burner on underneath it. Satisfied, she wandered into the main shop.

It wasn't large—but then Jessica had never intended it to be. Intimate, personal. Yes, it was that, she thought, with her signature on it. The shop was more than a business to her; it was an accomplishment, and a love. The business end—invoices, filing, books—she ran meticulously. All of her organizational efforts went into the shop, which perhaps was the reason for her lack of order elsewhere.

The shop was the focus of her life, and had been since she'd conceived of it. Initially she'd needed something to give some purpose to her life after college was behind her. The idea for the shop had germinated slowly, then had grown and developed. Jessica had too much drive, too much energy, to drift. Once she had decided to start a business, she'd moved quickly. Then that same drive and energy had made it work. It turned a profit. The money itself meant little, but the fact that her shop made it, meant everything.

She'd spent six months scouring New England, then Europe, for the right pieces. A large inventory hadn't been her goal, but an exclusive one. After her opening the response had begun as a small trickle, mostly friends and friends of friends. Justice Winslow's daughter running a shop had brought out the curiosity seekers as well. Jessica hadn't minded. A client was a client, and a satisfied one, the best advertising.

For the first two years she'd run the shop alone. Indeed, she had never considered that her business would outgrow her. When it had, she'd hired Michael Adams to handle the overseas buying. He was charming, capable, and knowledgeable. The women customers adored him. Gradually their relationship had mellowed from business to friendship to easy affection.

As business had continued to thrive, Jessica had hired David Ryce. He'd been hardly more than a boy, at loose ends, bored enough to find trouble if it got in his way. Jessica had hired him because they'd grown up together; then she had come to depend on him. He was quick with figures and tireless with details. He had a streak of street sense that made him a good man to have in business.

Street sense, Jessica mused. James Sladerman. Odd that the term would bring him back to her mind. Even in that quick exchange at the foot of the stairs, she'd felt something in him. It told her he was a man who would know how to handle himself—in business, maybe. In an alley, definitely. With a half laugh, she stuck her hands in her pockets. Now why should she think that?

The fingers that had gripped her arm had been strong. His build had been wiry. But no, it had been his eyes, she thought. There was something . . . hard in his eyes. Yet she hadn't been repelled or frightened, but drawn. Even when he'd looked at her for those first three or four seconds, with that intensity that seemed to creep beneath her skin, she hadn't been afraid. Safe, she realized. He'd made her feel safe.

That was odd, Jessica decided, catching her bottom lip between her teeth. Why should she suddenly feel safe when she had no need for protection?

The door of the shop jingled open. Pushing speculation aside, Jessica turned.

"Miss Winslow, I apologize. I'm very late."

"Don't give it a thought, Mr. Chambers." Jessica considered telling him that she'd also been late, then decided against it. What he didn't know wouldn't hurt him. Behind her, the kettle whistled. "I'm just making tea. Why don't you join me before we look over the new snuffboxes?"

Chambers removed a rather fussy hat from a balding head. "Wonderful. I do appreciate you calling me when you get a new shipment in." He smiled, revealing good dentures.

"You don't think I'd let anyone see the snuffboxes before you." In the kitchen Jessica poured boiling water into cups. "Michael found these in France. There are two I think you'll be particularly interested in."

He preferred the ornate, Jessica thought with a smile as she lifted the tray. He loved the foolishly gaudy little boxes that men with lace cuffs used to carry. She glanced at Chambers' stubby form and wondered if he pictured himself as a cavalier or perhaps a Regency buck. Still, his fascination with snuffboxes had made him a regular customer who had more than once recommended her shop to other people. And he was rather sweet in his fussy little way, she thought as she placed the tea tray on a table.

"Sugar?" she asked him.

"Ah, I shouldn't." Chambers patted his ample middle. "But perhaps one cube." His glance flicked briefly down to her legs as Jessica crossed them. A pity, he thought with an inward sigh, that he wasn't twenty years younger.

Later he left happily with two eighteenth-century snuffboxes. Before Jessica could file the invoice, she heard the grumble of an engine. Glancing up, she saw the large delivery truck pull in front of the shop. She read the company logo on the side of the steel doors and frowned a bit. She could have sworn the delivery that Michael was shipping wasn't due until the following day.

When she recognized the driver, Jessica waved, then walked to the front door to meet him.

"Hi, Miss Winslow."

"Hello, Don." She accepted the itemized list he handed her, muttering about not expecting him until tomorrow. He shrugged.

"Mr. Adams put a rush on it."

"Mmm." She jiggled the keys in her pocket as she scanned the list. "Well, he seems to have outdone himself this time. And another delivery on Saturday. I don't . . . oh!" Her eyes lit up with pleasure as they fixed on one item. "The writing desk. The Queen Anne. I meant to tell Michael to keep his eyes open for one, then forgot. It must be fate." Of course, she should uncart it first, at least take a look. No, impulses were the best, Jessica decided. Smiling, she looked back up at the driver. "The rest comes in here, but that goes to my home. Would you mind?"

"Well . . ."

It was easy to justify using the smile. Jessica could already see the desk in the front parlor. "If it's not too much trouble," she added.

The driver shifted to his other foot. "I guess it'll be all right. Joe won't mind." He jerked his thumb at his partner, who had opened the wide double doors of the truck.

"Thanks. I really appreciate it. That desk is just what I've been looking for."

Feeling triumphant, Jessica went to the back room for more tea.

As she had burst out hours before, Jessica burst in through the front door of the house. "Betsy!" She slung her purse over the newel post. "Did it come?" Without waiting for an answer, she dashed toward the front parlor.

"Since you were six, I've been telling you to slow down." Betsy came through the parlor doors, intercepting her. "At least then you wore sensible shoes."

"Betsy." Jessica gave her a quick, hard squeeze that held as much impatience as affection. "Did it come?"

"Yes, of course it came." The housekeeper straightened her apron with a tug. "And it's sitting in the parlor just like you told me. It'll be there whether you walk sensibly or run like a fool." The last of the sentence was wasted, as Jessica was already rushing by her.

"Oh, it's lovely!" Gently, she ran a finger over the wood, then quickly began to examine it on all sides. It was a delicate, airy little piece. A woman's desk. Jessica opened the slant top, then sighed at the

unmarred interior. "Really lovely. Wait until David
sees it." She opened one of the inner drawers. It slid
out smoothly. "It's exactly what I've been looking for.
What luck that Michael came across it." Crouching,
she ran a hand down one of its slender legs.

"It's pretty," Betsy admitted, thinking that the
carving would be one more thing to keep dust out of.
"I bet you could have sold it for a pretty penny too."

"The advantage of owning a shop is being able to
cop some of the merchandise for yourself." Rising,
Jessica shut the lid again. Now all she needed was a
frivolous little inkwell, or perhaps a porcelain box to
set on top of it.

"Supper's nearly ready."

"Oh, supper." Shaking her head, Jessica brought
herself back to the moment. "Mr. Sladerman, I've
neglected him all day. Is he upstairs?"

"In the library," Betsy announced grimly. "All day.
Wouldn't even come out for lunch."

"Oh boy." Jessica combed a hand through her hair.
He hadn't looked like a man who would have much
patience with disorganization. "I really wanted to
ease him into that. Well, I'm going to go be charming
so we don't lose him. What's for supper?" she asked
over her shoulder.

"Stuffed pork chops and mashed potatoes."

"That should help," Jessica muttered as she headed
for the library door.

She opened it slowly, enough to stick her head
inside. Some things, she decided, you don't rush into.
He was sitting at a long work table, surrounded by
pillars and piles of books. A thick pad was in front of

him, and the pencil in his hand was worked halfway down. His hair fell over his forehead, but she could see his brows drawn together in concentration. Or annoyance, she mused. She put on her best smile.

"Hi."

He looked up, eyes pinning her. Jessica could feel the little prickles of power all over her skin. She absorbed it, intrigued by the sensation. Without being aware of it, her smile had faded into a look of puzzlement.

Who is this man? she wondered. It was curiosity as much as courage that had her coming all the way into the room. The lamp on the desk slanted across his face, highlighting his mouth and putting his eyes in shadow. She didn't feel safe with him this time, but unsettled. She continued toward him.

"You've got a hell of a mess here," Slade said shortly, tossing his pencil aside. It was better to attack than let himself dwell on how beautiful she was. "If you run your shop like this"—he gestured widely— "it's a miracle you're not bankrupt."

The specific complaint eased the tension in her shoulders. There'd been nothing personal in that look, she assured herself. She'd been foolish to think there had been. "I know it's terrible," Jessica admitted, smiling again. "I hope you're not going to do the sensible thing and walk out." Gingerly, she lowered a hip to the table before lifting a book at random. "Do you like challenges, Mr. Sladerman?"

She was laughing, he noted. Or her eyes were. But he sensed very clearly that she laughed at herself. A reluctant smile tugged at his mouth as he struggled to study her objectively. Maybe she was innocent—maybe not. He didn't have the same blind faith as the commissioner. But she was beautiful, and he was attracted. Slade decided the attraction was going to be difficult to work around.

Letting out a long breath, he gazed around the room. How much choice did he have? "I'm going to take pity on you, Miss Winslow . . . I have a fondness for books."

"So do I," she began, then had to deal with another of his cool, direct looks. "Really," she claimed with a laugh. "I'm just not neat. Do we have a deal, Mr. Sladerman?" Solemnly, she offered her hand.

He glanced at it first. Soft and elegant, he thought, like her name and her voice. With a quick curse at fate for making the commissioner her godfather, Slade took her hand in his. "We have a deal, Miss Winslow."

Jessica slid from the table, keeping his hand in hers when he would have drawn away. Somehow she'd known it would be hard and strong. "How do you feel about stuffed pork chops?"

They were tender and delicious. Slade ate three after his stomach remembered the lack of lunch. And, he thought after a slice of cheesecake, this case had some advantages over the one he'd just wrapped up. For two weeks he'd made do on cold coffee and stale sandwiches. And his partner hadn't been as easy to look at as Jessica Winslow. She'd guided the conversation expertly during the meal and had ended by tucking her arm through his to lead him back to the parlor.

"Have a seat," she invited. "I'll pour you a brandy."

As he started to cross the room the desk caught his eye. "That wasn't here this morning."

"What?" With a decanter in her hand, she glanced over her shoulder. "Oh no, it just came this afternoon. Do you know anything about antiques?"

"No." He gave the desk a cursory study before taking a chair. "I'll leave that to you, Miss Winslow."

"Jessica." She poured a second brandy before crossing to him. "Do I call you James or Jim?"

"Slade," he told her as he took a snifter. "Even my mother stopped calling me Jim when I was ten."

"You have a mother?"

The quick, unconscious surprise in her voice had him grinning. "Everybody's entitled to one."

Feeling foolish, Jessica sat across from him. "You just seem to be capable of arranging the whole business without one."

Both sipped brandy, and their eyes met over the snifters. Jessica felt the moment freeze, out of time, out of place. Do minds touch? she thought numbly. Wasn't she sensing at that moment the turbulent spin of his thoughts? Or were they hers? Brandy slipped, hot and strong down her throat, snapping her back. Talk, she ordered herself. Say something. "Do you have any other family?" she managed.

Slade stared at her, wondering if he had imagined that instant of stunning intimacy. He'd never felt that with any woman before, any lover. It was ridiculous to imagine that he'd felt it with one he barely knew. "A sister," he said at length. "She's in college."

"A sister." Jessica relaxed again and slipped out of her shoes. "That's nice. I always wanted a brother or sister when I was growing up."

"Money can't buy everything." Slade shrugged with the words. Seeing the puzzled hurt on her face, he cursed himself. If she was getting to him already, what would it be like in a week?

"You're quick with clichés," Jessica observed. "I suppose that's because you're a writer." After another sip of brandy, she set the glass aside. "What do you write?"

"Unpublished novels."

She laughed as she had in the library, drawing another smile from him. "It must be frustrating."

"Only daily," he agreed.

"Why do you do it?"

"Why do you eat?"

Jessica considered for a moment, then nodded. "Yes, I suppose it's like that, isn't it? Have you always wanted to write?"

He thought of his father, how he had bragged that his son would be the next Sladerman on the force. He thought of his teenage years, when he had written his stories in longhand in spiral notebooks late into the night. He thought of his father's eyes the first time he had seen his son in uniform. And he thought of the first time he'd had a short story accepted.

"Yes." Perhaps it was easier to admit to her what he had never been able to explain to his family. "Always."

"When you want something badly enough, and you don't give up," Jessica began slowly, "you get it."

Slade gave a short laugh before he drank. "Always?"

She touched the tip of her tongue to her top lip. "Almost always. It's all a gamble, isn't it?"

"Long odds," he murmured, frowning into his glass. "I usually play long odds." He studied the amber liquor, which was almost exactly the shade of her eyes. She shouldn't be so easy to talk to, he mused. He'd find himself saying too much.

"Ah, Ulysses, I wondered where you were."

Lifting his eyes, Slade stared at a large, loping mop of fur. It lunged, unerringly, into Jessica's lap. He heard her groan, then giggle.

"Damn it! How many times do I have to tell you you're not a lap dog. You're breaking my ribs." She twisted her head, but the wet, pink tongue found her cheek. "Stop!" she sputtered, pushing impotently. "Get down," she ordered. "Get down right this minute." Ulysses barked twice, then continued to lap his tongue all over her face.

"What," Slade asked slowly, "is that?"

Jessica gave another mighty shove, but Ulysses only rested his head on her shoulder. "A dog, of course."

"There's no 'of course' about that dog."

"He's a Great Pyrenees," she retorted, quickly running out of breath. "And he flunked obedience school three times. You mangy, soft-headed mutt, get down." Ulysses let out a long, contented breath and didn't budge. "Give me a hand, will you?" she demanded of Slade. "I'll have internal injuries this time. Once before I was stuck for two hours until Betsy got home."

Rising, Slade approached the dog with a frown. "Does he bite?"

"God, I'm suffocating and the man asks if he bites."

A grin split Slade's face as he looked down at her. "Can't be too careful about these things. He might be vicious."

Jessica narrowed her eyes. "Sic 'em, Ulysses!" Hearing his name, the dog roused himself to lick her face again, joyfully. "Satisfied?" Jessica demanded. "Now grab him somewhere and get me out."

Bending, Slade wrapped his arms around the bulk of fur. The back of his hand brushed Jessica's breast as he shifted his grip. "Sorry," he muttered, dragging at the dog. "Good God, what does he weigh?"

"About one twenty-five, I think."

With a shake of his head, Slade put his back into it. Ulysses slid to the floor to lay adoringly at Jessica's feet. Taking a deep gulp of air, Jessica closed her eyes.

She was covered with loose white hair. Her own was disheveled and curled around her shoulders, the color, Slade observed, of sun-bleached wheat. With her face in repose, the slant of her cheekbones was more pronounced. Her lips were just parted. Their shape was utterly feminine—the classic cupid's bow but for the fullness in the lower lip. It spoke of passion—hidden, quietly simmering passion. The mouth and the cheekbones added something to the tearoom looks that had Slade's pulse responding. He couldn't want her, he told himself. That wasn't just irresponsible, it was stupid. He stared down at the dog again.

"You should do something about training him," he said shortly.

"I know." With a sigh, Jessica opened her brandy-colored eyes. Her affection for Ulysses made her forget the discomfort and the mess he usually created. "He's very sensitive really. I just haven't got the heart to subject him to obedience school again."

"That's incredibly stupid," Slade tossed back. "He's too big not to be trained."

"Want the job?" Jessica retorted. Straightening in the chair, she began to brush at stray dog hair.

"I've got one, thanks."

Why should it annoy her that he hadn't once used her name? she asked herself as she rose. Dignity had to be sacrificed as she stepped over the now sleeping dog. "I appreciate the help," she said stiffly. "And the advice is duly noted."

Slade shrugged off the sarcasm. "No problem. You struck me as more the poodle type, though."

"Really?" For a moment Jessica merely studied his eyes. Yes, they were hard, she decided. Hard and cool and cynical. "And I have the impression you don't think much of the poodle type. Help yourself to the brandy. I'm going up."

Chapter 2

FOR THE NEXT TWO DAYS THERE WAS AN UNEASY TRUCE. Perhaps it lasted that long because Jessica made a point of staying out of Slade's way. He in turn stayed out of hers while patiently noting her routine—which, he discovered, was no routine at all. She simply never stopped. She didn't take time for the social rigamarole he had expected—luncheons, clubs, committees—but worked, apparently inexhaustibly. Most of her time was spent at the shop. At the rate he was going, he knew he would find out little in the house. His next move was the House of Winslow. It followed that he needed to make peace with Jessica to get there.

From his bedroom window, he watched her drive away. It was barely eight o'clock, a full hour before she normally left. Slade swore in frustration. How did the commissioner expect him to watch her—or protect her if that's what she needed—if she was always in one place while he was in another? It was time to improvise an excuse to pay her a visit at her place of business.

Grabbing a jacket on the way, Slade headed for the stairs. He could always claim that he wanted to do a bit of research on antique furniture for his novel. That would buy him a few hours, as well as give him a reason to poke around. Before he'd rounded the last curve in the steps he heard Betsy's voice.

". . . nothing but trouble."

"Don't fuss."

Slade stopped, waiting as the footsteps came his way. There was a tall, gangly man walking down the hall. His mop of dark blond hair was long and straight, cut rather haphazardly just below the collar of a chambray workshirt. He wore jeans and wire-rim glasses and stood hunched over a bit—either from habit or fatigue. Because he was staring down at his sneakers, he didn't see Slade. His face was pale and the eyes behind the lenses were shadowed. David Ryce, Slade concluded, and kept silent.

"I told you she said you weren't to come in today." Betsy bustled after him, a feather duster gripped in her hand.

"I'm fine. If I lie around in bed another day, I'm going to mold." He coughed violently.

"Fine, fine indeed." Betsy clucked her tongue, swinging the duster at his back.

"Mom, lay off." Exasperated, David started to turn back to her when he spotted Slade. He frowned, choking back another cough. "Oh, you must be the writer."

"That's right." Slade came down the last two steps.

Just a boy, he thought, taking David's measure quickly. Who hasn't completely thrown off the youthful defiance.

"Jessie and I figured you'd be a short, stooped little guy with glasses. I don't know why." He grinned, but Slade noted that he placed a hand on the newel post for support. "Getting anywhere with the library?"

"Slowly."

"Better you than me," David murmured, wishing for a chair. "Has Jessica come down yet?"

"She's already gone," Slade told him.

"There, you see." Betsy folded her arms over her chest. "And if you go in, she'll just send you right back home. Thunder at you too."

Because his legs threatened to buckle, David gripped the newel post harder. "She's going to need help with the new shipment. Another's due in today."

"Lotta good you'd do," Betsy began. Catching the look in David's eye, Slade cut in.

"I was thinking about running down there myself. I'd like to see the place, maybe do a little research. I could give her a hand." He watched David struggle, caught between his desire to go to the shop and his need to lie down.

"She'll try to move everything herself," he muttered.

"That's the truth," Betsy agreed, apparently switching her annoyance from her son to her employer. "Nothing stops that one."

"It's my job to move in the new stock, check it off. I don't—"

"Moving furniture around shouldn't require any

great knowledge of antiques," Slade put in casually. Knowing it was too perfect to let pass, he slipped into his jacket. "And since I was heading that way anyway . . ."

"There, it's settled," Betsy announced. She had her son by the elbow before he could protest. "Mr. Sladerman will go look out for Miss Jessica. You go back to bed."

"I'm not going back to bed. A chair, all I want's a chair." He sent Slade a weak smile. "Hey, thanks. Tell Jessie I'm coming back on Monday. The paperwork on the new stock can wait over the weekend. Tell her to humor the invalid and leave it for me."

Slade nodded slowly. "Sure, I'll tell her." Turning, he started out, deciding that the new stock interested him very much.

Fifteen minutes later Slade parked in the small graveled lot beside Jessica's shop. It was a small, framed building, fronted with several narrow windows. The shades were up. Through the glass, he could see her tugging on a large and obviously heavy piece of furniture. Cursing women in general, he walked to the front door and pulled it open.

At the jingle of bells she spun around. That anyone would be by the shop at that hour surprised her—that Slade stood inside the door frowning at her surprised Jessica more. "Well . . ." The physical exertion had winded her so that she struggled to even her breathing. "I didn't expect to see you here." She didn't add that she wasn't particularly pleased either.

She'd stripped off her jacket and pushed up the sleeves of her cashmere sweater. Beneath it, small high breasts rose and fell agitatedly. Slade remembered their softness against the back of his hand very clearly. He forgot he'd come to make peace with her.

"Don't you have more sense than to push this stuff around yourself?" he demanded. With a quick oath, he pulled off his jacket and tossed it over a chair. Jessica stiffened her back as well as her tone.

"Well, good morning to you too."

Her annoyance rolled off of him. After crossing to her, Slade leaned against the large piece she'd been struggling with. "Where do you want it?" he asked shortly. "And I hope to God you're not one of those women who changes her mind a half dozen times."

He watched her eyes narrow and darken as they had that night in the parlor. Oddly, he found her only more attractive when she was agitated. If it hadn't been for that, the way her chin jutted out might have amused him. "I don't believe anyone asked for your assistance." For the first time he was treated to the ice in her tone. "I'm capable of arranging my stock myself."

"Don't be any more stupid than necessary," he shot back. "You're just going to hurt yourself. Now where do you want this thing?"

"This *thing*," she began heatedly, "is a nineteenth-century French secretaire."

He gave it a negligent glance. "Yeah, so? Where do you want me to put it?"

"I'll tell you where you can put it—"

His laughter cut her off. It was very male and full of fun. It wasn't a sound she had expected from him. With an effort, she swallowed a chuckle of her own as she stepped back from him. The last thing she wanted was to find anything appealing about James Sladerman. "Over there," she said coolly, pointing. Turning away, Jessica picked up a washstand to carry it in the opposite direction. When the sounds of wood sliding over wood had stopped, she turned back to him.

"Thank you." The gratitude was short and cold. "Now, what can I do for you?"

He treated himself to a lengthy look at her. She stood very straight, her hands folded loosely, her eyes still dangerous. Two mother-of-pearl combs swept her hair back from her face. He allowed his gaze to sweep down briefly. She was very slender, with a hand-spanable waist and barely any hips. The trim flannel skirt hid most of her legs, but Slade could appreciate what was visible from the knees down. Her feet were very small. One of them tapped the floor impatiently.

"I've thought about that from time to time," he commented as his eyes roamed back to hers. "But I came by to see what I could do for you. Ryce was worried that you might do just what you were trying to do a few minutes ago."

"You've seen David?" Her cool impatience evaporated. Swiftly, Jessica crossed the room to take Slade's arm. "Was he up? How is he?"

Suddenly he wanted to touch her—her hair, her face. She'd be soft. He felt an almost desperate need for something soft and yielding. Her eyes were on his, wide with concern. "He was up," he said briefly. "And not as well as he wanted to be."

"He shouldn't have been out of bed."

"No, probably not." Did her hair carry that scent? he wondered. That autumn-woods fragrance that was driving him mad? "He wanted to come in this morning."

"Come in?" Jessica pounced on the two words. "I gave specific orders for him to stay home. Why can't he do as he's told?"

Slade's eyes were suddenly keen on her face. "Does everyone do what you tell them?"

"He's my employee," she retorted, dropping her hand from his arm. "He damn well better do what I tell him." As quickly as she had flared up, her mood shifted and she smiled. "He's hardly more than a boy really, and Betsy nags at him. It's just her way. Though I appreciate his dedication to the business, he's got to get well." Her eyes drifted to the phone on the counter. "If I call, he'll just get defensive."

"He said he wouldn't come in until Monday." Slade leaned against the secretaire. "He wanted you to leave the paperwork on the new shipments for him."

Jessica stuck her hands in her pockets, obviously still toying with the idea of phoning to lecture David. "Yes, all right. If he's going to come in on Monday, at least he'll be sitting down. I'll get the new stock situated in the meantime so he's not tempted." She smiled again. "He's nearly as obsessed with this place as I am. If I so much as move a candlestick, David knows it. Before he got sick, he was trying to talk me into a vacation." She laughed, tossing her head so that her hair swung behind her. "He just wanted the place to himself for a week or two."

"A very dedicated assistant," Slade murmured.

"Oh, David's that," Jessica agreed. "What are you

doing here, Slade? I thought you'd be buried in books."

Half glad, half wary that the reserve of the last few days had vanished, he gave her a cautious smile. "I told David I'd give you a hand."

"That was very nice." The surprise in her voice had his smile widening.

"I can be nice occasionally," he returned. "Besides, I thought I might be able to get some information on antiques. Research."

"Oh." She accepted this with a nod. "All right. I wouldn't mind having some help with the heavier things. What period were you interested in?"

"Period?"

"Furniture," Jessica explained as she walked to a long, low chest. "Is there a particular century or style? Renaissance, Early American, Italian Provincial?"

"Just a general sort of lesson today to give me the feel of it," Slade improvised as he nudged Jessica away from the chest. "Where do you want this?"

He lifted and carried. Jessica arranged the lighter pieces while keeping up a running dialog on the furniture they moved. This chair was a Chippendale—see the square, tapered seat and cabriole leg. This cabinet was French Baroque—in satinwood, gilded and carved. She ran over a little table with a polishing cloth, explaining about Chinese influences and tea services.

During the morning they were interrupted half a dozen times by customers. Jessica turned from antique lover to salesperson. Slade watched her show pieces, explain their background, then dicker over prices. If he hadn't been sure before, he was certain now. Her shop was no toy to her. She not only knew how to manage it, but worked harder than he'd given her credit for. Not only did she handle people with a deft skill he was forced to admire, but she made money—if the discreet price tags he'd come across were any indication.

So why, he wondered, if she was dedicated to her shop, if she turned a profit, would she risk using her business for smuggling? Now that he'd met her and spent some time with her, it wasn't as easy for Slade to dismiss it as kicks or thrills. Yet she wasn't lacking in brains. Was it plausible that an operation was going on under her nose without her knowledge?

"Slade, I hate to ask." Jessica kept her voice lowered as she came close to his side. Touching came naturally to her, it seemed, for her hand was already on his arm. Irresponsible or not, he discovered that he wanted her. Turning, he trapped her effectively between the chest and himself. Her hand remained on his arm, just below the elbow. Though they touched in no other way, he suddenly had a very clear sensation of how her body would feel pressed against his. His eyes brushed over her mouth, then came to hers.

"Ask what?"

Her mind went blank. Some sound filled her head, like an echo of surf pounding on the shore. She could have stepped back an inch and broken the contact— stepped forward an inch to consummate it. Jessica did neither. Dimly, she was aware of a pressure in her chest, as though someone were pressing hard against it to cut off her air. In that instant they both knew he had only to touch her for everything to change.

"Slade," she murmured. Half question, half invitation.

He snapped back, retreating from the edge, from an involvement he couldn't afford. "Did you want me to move something else?" His voice was cool as he stepped away from her.

Shaken, Jessica backed toward the chest. She needed distance. "Mrs. MacKenzie wants to take the chifforobe with her. She's gone out to pull her car to the front. Would you mind putting it in the back of her station wagon?"

"All right."

She indicated the piece with a silent gesture, not moving until he was out the front door with it. Alone, Jessica allowed herself a long, uneasy breath. That was not a man a woman should lose control with, she warned herself. He wouldn't be gentle, or particularly kind. She placed the flat of her palm on her chest as if to relieve the pressure that lingered there. Don't overreact the next time, she advised herself.

It's the way he looks at me, Jessica decided, as if he could see what I'm thinking. She ran an unsteady hand through her hair. I don't even know what I'm thinking when he looks at me, so how could he? And yet . . . and yet her pulse was still racing.

When the door jingled open again, she hadn't budged from her spot in front of the chest of drawers.

"I'm starved," she improvised swiftly, then started to move. As Slade watched she hurried from window to window, lowering shades. She hung a sign on the door and then locked it. "You must be too," she said when he remained silent. "It's after one, and I've had you dragging furniture around all morning. How about a sandwich and some tea?"

Slade managed to smile and sneer at the same time. "Tea?"

Her laughter eased her own tension. "No, I suppose not. Well, David keeps some beer." She hustled to the back of the shop and pulled open the door of a small refrigerator. She crouched, then rummaged. "Here. I knew I'd seen some." Straightening, Jessica turned and collided with his chest. He took her arms briefly in reflex, then as quickly dropped them. Heart hammering, she stepped away. "Sorry, I didn't know you were behind me. Will this do?" Safely at arm's length, she offered the bottle.

"Fine." His expression was bland as he took it and sat at the table. The tension had settled at the base of his neck. He'd have to be careful not to touch her again. Or to give in to the urge to taste that subtly passionate mouth of hers. Once he did, he'd never stop there. Desire tightened, a hard ball in the pit of his stomach. Almost violently, Slade twisted the cap from the beer.

"I'll fix some sandwiches." Jessica became very busy in the refrigerator. "Roast beef all right?"

"Yeah, that's fine."

What goes on in his mind? she wondered as she kept her hands busy. It's just not possible to tell what he's thinking. She sliced neatly through bread and meat, prudently keeping her back to him. Looking down at her own hands, she thought of Slade's. He had such long, lean fingers. Strong. She'd liked the look of them. Now, she caught herself wondering how they would feel on her body. Competent, experienced, demanding. The flare of desire was quick, but not unexpected this time. Fighting it, she sliced the second sandwich a bit savagely.

He watched the sunlight stream through the window onto her hair. It fell softly on the varied hues of blue in her sweater. He liked the way the material clung to her, enhancing the straight, slender back and narrow waist. But he noted too the tension in her shoulders. He wasn't going to get very far if they were both preoccupied with an attraction neither wanted. He had to make her relax and talk. Slade knew one certain way of accomplishing that.

"You've got quite a place here, Jessica."

He wasn't aware that it was the first time he'd said her name, but she was. That pleased her as much as the careful compliment.

"Thank you." Belatedly she remembered to turn the burner on under the kettle as she brought his sandwich to the table. "People have finally stopped calling it Jessica's Little Hobby."

"Is that what it started out to be?"

"Not to me." She stretched on tiptoe to reach a cup. Slade watched the hem of her skirt sneak up. "But to a lot of people it was just Justice Winslow's daughter having a fling at business. Did you want a glass for that?"

"No." Slade brought the bottle to his lips and drank. "Why antiques?"

"It was something I knew . . . something I loved.

It's sensible to make a career out of something you know and appreciate, don't you think?"

He thought of the standard police-issue revolver hidden in his bedroom. "When it's possible. How'd you get started?"

"I was lucky enough to have the funds to back me up the first year while I gathered stock and renovated this place." The kettle shrilled, then sputtered when she switched off the heat. "Even with that, it was hard enough. Setting up books, getting licenses, learning about taxes." She wrinkled her nose as she brought her plate and cup to the table. "But that's a necessary part of the whole. With that, the traveling, and the selling, the first couple of years were killers." She bit into her sandwich. "I loved it."

She would have, he mused. He could sense the pent-up energy even as she sat there calmly drinking tea. "David Ryce work for you long?"

"About a year and a half. He was at that undecided point of his life I suppose we all go through when we've finished being teenagers but haven't quite grasped adulthood." She smiled across the table at Slade. "Do you know what I mean?"

"More or less."

"You probably less than most," she commented easily. "As it turned out, he resented the offer of a job and the fact that he needed one. David and I grew up together. There's nothing harder on the ego than having big sister give you a break." She sighed a bit, remembering his moodiness, his grudging acceptance, his initial lack of interest. "Anyway, within six months he stopped being resentful and became indispensable. He's very quick, particularly with figures. David considers the books his province now. And he's better with them than the selling angle."

"Oh?"

Her eyes danced. "He isn't always . . . diplomatic with customers. He's much better with bookkeeping and inventory. Michael and I can handle the buying and selling."

"Michael." Before he drank again, Slade repeated the name as though it meant nothing.

"Michael does almost all my buying, all the imports at any rate."

"You don't buy the stock yourself?"

"Not from overseas, not anymore." Jessica toyed with the last half of her sandwich. "If I'd tried to keep up with it, I wouldn't have been able to keep the shop open year round. Watching out for estate sales and auctions just in the New England area takes me away from the shop enough as it is. And Michael . . . Michael has a real genius for finding gems."

He wondered if her analogy was fact. Was Michael Adams shipping gems as well as Hepplewhites across the Atlantic?

"Michael's been handling that part of the business for nearly three years," Jessica went on. "And he's not only a good buyer, but a terrific salesman. Particularly with my female clientele." She laughed as she lifted her cup. "He's very smooth—both looks and manner."

Slade noted the affection in her voice and speculated. Just how much was between owner and buyer? he wondered. If Adams was involved in smuggling, and Jessica's lover. . . . His thoughts trailed off as he looked down at her hands. She wore a thin, twisted band of gold on her right hand and a star-shaped group of opals on her left. The sun hit the stones, shooting little flames of red into the delicate blue. It suited her, he thought, taking another swig of beer.

"In any case, I've gotten spoiled." Jessica stretched her shoulders with a sigh. "It's been a long time since I've had to run the shop alone. I'll be glad to have both Michael and David back next week. I might even take Uncle Charlie up on his invitation."

"Uncle Charlie?"

Her cup paused halfway to her lips. "Uncle Charlie," Jessica repeated, puzzled. "He sent you."

Slade gave a quick silent oath as he shrugged. "The commissioner," he said blandly. "I don't think of him as Uncle Charlie."

"The commissioner's awfully formal." Still frowning at him, Jessica set down her cup.

She's not a fool, Slade concluded as he swung an arm over the back of his chair. "I always call him that. Habit. Don't you like to travel?" He changed the subject neatly, adding a quick, disarming smile. "I'd think the buying end would be half the fun."

"It can be. It can also be a giant headache. Airports and auctions and customs." The line between her brows vanished. "I have been thinking about combining a business and pleasure trip next spring. I want to visit my mother and her husband in France."

"Your mother remarried?"

"Yes, it's been wonderful for her. After my father died, she was so lost. We both were," she murmured. And after nearly five years, she mused, there was still an ache. It was dull with time, but it was still there.

"There's nothing harder than to lose someone you loved and lived with and depended on. Especially when you think that person is indestructible; then he's taken away with no warning."

Her voice had thickened, touching off a chord of response in him. "I know," he answered before he thought.

Her eyes came up and fixed on his. "Do you?"

He didn't like the emotion she stirred up in him. "My father was a cop," he answered curtly. "He was killed in action five years ago."

"Oh, Slade." Jessica reached for his hand. "How terrible—how terrible for your mother."

"Wives of cops learn to live with the risk." He moved his hand back to his beer.

Sensing withdrawal, Jessica said nothing. He wasn't a man to share emotion of any kind easily. She rose, stacking plates. "Do you want something else? I imagine there're cookies stashed around here somewhere."

She wouldn't probe, he realized, wouldn't eulogize. She'd offered him her sympathy, then had backed off when she'd seen that it wasn't wanted. Slade sighed. It was difficult enough to deal with his attraction to her without starting to like her as well.

"No." He rose to help her clear the table.

When they entered the shop, Jessica went straight to the door to snap up the shade on the glass. Slade whirled sharply as he heard her quick cry of alarm. It was immediately followed by a laugh. "Mr. Layton." Jessica flipped the lock to admit him. "You scared the wits out of me."

He was tall, well dressed, and fiftyish. His bankerish suit was offset by a gray silk tie the same color as his hair. The rather thin, stern face lightened with a smile as he took Jessica's hand. "Sorry, dear, but then, you did the same to me." Glancing past her, he gave Slade an inquiring look.

"This is James Sladerman, Mr. Layton. He's staying with us for a while. David's been ill."

"Oh, nothing serious, I hope."

"Just the flu," Jessica told him. "But a heavy dose of it." She gave him a sudden shrewd smile. "You always manage to pop in on me when I've just gotten in a shipment. I've just managed to get this one arranged, and another's on its way."

He chuckled, a hoarse sound due to his fondness for Cuban cigars. "It's more your predictability than chance, Miss Winslow. Your Michael's been in Europe for three weeks. I'd asked him to keep an eye out for a piece or two for me before he left."

"Oh, well—" The jingle of the door interrupted her. "Mr. Chambers, I didn't expect you back so soon."

Chambers gave her a rather sheepish smile as he removed his hat. "The box with the pearl inlay," he began. "I can't resist it."

"Go on ahead, my dear." Layton gave Jessica's shoulder a pat. "I'll just browse for the moment."

Pretending an interest in a collection of pewter, Slade watched both men. Layton browsed, lingering here and there to examine a piece. Once he drew out a pair of half glasses and crouched down to study the carving on a table. Slade could hear Jessica's quiet voice as she discussed a snuffbox with Chambers. He choked back a snort of derision at the idea of a rational man buying anything as ridiculous as a snuffbox. After telling Jessica to wrap the box, Chambers turned to fuss over a curio cabinet.

It was a simple matter for Slade to mentally note both men's descriptions and names. Later he would commit them to paper and call them in. Whoever they were, they appeared to have at least a basic knowledge of antiques—at least from what he could glean from their conversation as they both discussed the cabinet. Wandering to the counter, Slade glanced down at the ticket Jessica was writing up. Her handwriting was neat, feminine, and legible.

One eighteenth-century snuffbox. French with pearl inlay.

It was the price that had him doing a double take. "Are you kidding?" he said aloud.

"Ssh!" She glanced over at her customers, saw that they were occupied, then sent Slade a wicked grin. "Don't you have any vices, Slade?"

"Immoral, not insane," he retorted, but the grin had appealed to him. He leaned a bit closer. "Do you?"

She let the look hold, enjoying the easy humor in his eyes. It was the first time she'd seen it. "No." She gave a low laugh. "Absolutely none."

For the first time he reached out to touch her voluntarily—just the tip of her hair with the tip of his finger. The pen slipped out of Jessica's hand. "Are you corruptible?" he murmured. He was still smiling, but she no longer felt easy. Jessica found herself grateful that the counter was between them and there were customers in the shop.

"I wouldn't have thought so," she managed. Layton's hoarse chuckle distracted her. Coming around the counter, Jessica walked toward her customers, giving Slade a wide berth.

Dangerous curves ahead, her mind warned. One wrong turn with this man and you'd be through the guardrail and over the cliff. She'd been too cautious for too long to be reckless now.

"It's a lovely little piece," she said to both men. "It arrived right after you'd left the other day, Mr. Chambers." She was aware, though he made no sound, when Slade turned his attention from her and wandered to the far end of the room.

In the end Chambers bought the cabinet, while Layton chose what Jessica referred to as a fauteuil and a console from the Louis XV period. Slade saw them as a chair and a table, too ornate for the average taste. But elegant names, he imagined, equaled elegant prices.

"With customers like that," he commented when the shop was empty, "you could open a place twice this size."

"I could," she agreed as she filed the slips. "But it's not what I want. And, of course, not everyone buys as freely. Those are men who know what they like and can afford to have it. It's my good fortune that they've taken to buying it here for the past year or so."

She watched him poke around, opening a drawer here and there until he settled in front of a corner cabinet. Inside was a collection of porcelain figures.

"Lovely, aren't they?" she commented as she joined him.

He kept his back to her, though that didn't prevent her scent from creeping into his senses. "Yeah, they're nice." She caught her bottom lip between her teeth. It wasn't often Dresden was described as *nice*. "My mother likes things like this."

"I've always thought this was the best in the collection." Jessica opened the door and drew out a small, delicate shepherdess. "I nearly whisked her away for myself."

Slade frowned at it. "She does have a birthday."

"And a thoughtful son." Her eyes were dancing when he lifted his to them.

"How much?" he said flatly.

Jessica ran her tongue over her teeth. It was bargaining time. There was nothing she liked better. "Twenty dollars," she said impulsively.

He laughed shortly. "I'm not stupid, Jessica. How much?"

When she tilted her head, the stubborn line appeared between her brows. "Twenty-two fifty. That's my last offer."

Reluctantly, he smiled. "You're crazy."

"Take it or leave it," she said with a shrug. "It's your mother's birthday after all."

"It's worth a hell of a lot more than that."

"It certainly would be to her," Jessica agreed.

Frustrated, Slade stuck his hands in his pockets and frowned at the figurine again. "Twenty-five," he said.

"Sold." Before he could change his mind, Jessica hustled over to the counter and began to box it. With a deft move, she peeled the price tag from the bottom and dropped it in the trash. "I can gift-wrap if you like," she said. "No charge."

Slowly he walked over to the counter, watching as she laid the porcelain in a bed of tissue paper. "Why?"

"Because it's her birthday. Birthday presents should be wrapped."

"That's not what I mean." He put a hand on the box to stop her movements. "Why?" he repeated.

Jessica gave him a long, considering look. He didn't like favors, she concluded, and only took this one because it was for someone he cared for. "Because I want to."

His brow lifted and his eyes were suddenly very intense. "Do you always do what you want?"

"I give it my best shot. Doesn't everyone?"

Before he could answer, the door opened again. "Delivery for you, Miss Winslow."

Slade felt a stir of excitement as the delivery was off-loaded. Maybe, just maybe, there'd be something. He wanted to tie this case up quickly, neatly, and be gone . . . while he still had some objectivity. Jessica Winslow had a way of smearing the issue. They weren't a man and woman, and he couldn't forget it. He was a cop, she was a suspect. His job was to find out what he could, even if it meant turning evidence on her. Listening to her steady stream of excitement as he uncarted boxes, Slade thought he'd never known anyone who appeared less capable of dishonesty. But that was a feeling, a hunch. He needed facts.

In his temporary position as mover and hauler, he was able to examine each piece carefully. He caught no uneasiness from Jessica, but rather her appreciation for helping her check for damage during shipping. The twinge of conscience infuriated him. He was doing his job, he reminded himself. And it was her damn Uncle Charlie that had put him there. Another year, Slade told himself again. Another year and there'd be no commissioner to hand him special assignments as a baby sitter cum spy for goddaughters with amber eyes.

He found nothing. His instinct had told him he wouldn't but Slade could have used even a crumb to justify his presence. She never stopped moving. For the two hours it took to unload the shipment, Jessica was everywhere, polishing, arranging, dragging out empty crates. When there was nothing more to do, she looked around for more.

"That's it," Slade told her before she could decide that something might be shown to a better advantage somewhere else.

"I guess you're right." Absently, she rubbed at the small of her back. "It's a good thing those three pieces are being shipped out Monday. It's a bit crowded. Hey, I'm starving." She turned to him with an apologetic smile. "I didn't mean to keep you so long, Slade. It's after five." Without giving him a chance to comment, she dashed to the back room for their jackets. "Here, I'll close up."

"How about a hamburger and a movie?" he said impulsively. I'm just keeping an eye on her, he told himself. That's what I'm here to do.

Surprised, Jessica glanced around as she pulled down the last shade. From the look on his face, she thought, amused, he was already half regretting having asked. But that was no reason to let him off the hook. "What a romantic invitation. How can I refuse?"

"You want romance?" he countered. "We'll go to a drive-in movie."

He heard her quick gurgle of laughter as he grabbed her hand and pulled her outside.

It was late when the phone rang. The seated figure reached for it and a cigarette simultaneously. "Hello."

"Where's the desk?"

"The desk?" Frowning, he brought the flame to the tip and drew. "It's with the rest of the shipment, of course."

"You're mistaken." The voice was soft and cold. "I've been to the shop myself."

"It has to be there." A flutter of panic rose in his throat. "Jessica just hasn't unpacked it yet."

"Possibly. You'll clear this up immediately. I want the desk and its contents by Wednesday." The pause was slight. "You understand the penalty for mistakes."

Chapter 3

JESSICA WOKE THINKING OF HIM. SHE TOOK TIME ON THE lazy Sunday morning to ponder the very odd Saturday she had spent—most of it with Slade. A moody man, she mused, stretching her arms toward the ceiling. By turns she had been comfortable with him, exasperated by him, and attracted to him. No, that wasn't quite true, she amended. Even when she'd been comfortable or exasperated, she'd been attracted. There was something remote about him that made her want to pry him open a bit. She'd put quite a lot of effort into that the evening before and had come up with nothing. He wasn't a man for divulging secrets or bothering with small talk. He was an odd combination of the direct and the aloof.

He didn't flatter—not by looks or words. And yet she felt certain that he wasn't indifferent to her. It wasn't possible that she'd imagined those moments of physical pull. They'd been there, for him as well as for her. But he had guards, she thought with quick frustration. She'd never known a man with such guards. Those dark, intense eyes of his clearly said "Keep back; arm's length." While the challenge of piercing his armor appealed to her, her own instinctive awareness of what the consequences would be held her back. Jessica enjoyed a dare, but she usually figured the odds first. In this case, she decided, they were stacked against her.

A nice, cautious friendship was in order, she concluded. Anything else spelled trouble. Rising, she picked up her robe and headed for the shower. But wouldn't it be nice, she thought, to feel that rather hard mouth on hers. Just once.

Downstairs, Slade was closeted in the library. He'd been up since dawn—she was crowding his mind. What crazy impulse had prompted him to ask her out the night before? After downing his fourth cup of coffee, Slade lit a cigarette. For God's sake, he didn't have to date the woman to do his job. She was getting to him, he admitted as he pushed a pile of books aside. That low, musical laugh and all that soft blond hair. It was more than that, he thought ruefully. It was her. She was too close to possessing all the things he'd ever wanted in a woman—warmth, generosity, intelligence. And that steamy, almost primitive sexuality you could sense just under the surface. If he kept thinking of her that way, it was going to cloud his objectivity. Even now he was finding himself trying to work out a way to keep her out of the middle.

When Slade drew on the cigarette, his eyes were

hard and opaque. He'd protect her when the time came, expose her if it came to that. But there was no way to keep her out of it. Still, over the mix of leather and dust and smoke, he thought he caught a lingering trace of her scent.

After evading the cook's admonishment to put something in her stomach, Jessica drank a hurried cup of coffee. "Where's David?" she called out when she spotted Betsy, armed with a rag and a bottle of silver polish.

"He took a walk down to the beach." His mother harrumphed a bit, but added, "He looks better. I guess the air'll do him good."

"I'll grab a jacket and check on him."

"Long as he doesn't know that's what you're up to."

"Betsy!" Jessica feigned offense. "I'm much too good for that." As the housekeeper snorted, the doorbell sounded. "Go ahead," Jessica told her. "I'll get it." She made a dash for the door. "Michael!" With pleasure, she threw her arms around his neck. "It's good to have you back."

Slade came into the hall in time to see Jessica embraced and kissed. With that low promising laugh, she pressed her cheek against the cheek of a slender, dark-haired man with smooth features and light green eyes. Michael Adams, Slade concluded, after conquering the urge to stride up to the couple and yank them apart. The description fit. He caught the gleam of a diamond on the man's pinky as he ran his hand through Jessica's hair. Soft hands and a sunlamp tan, Slade thought instantly.

"I've missed you, darling." Michael drew Jessica back far enough to smile into her face.

She laughed again, touching a hand to his cheek before she stepped out of his arms. "Knowing you, Michael, you were too busy with business and . . . other things to miss anyone. How many broken hearts did you leave in Europe?"

"I never break them," Michael claimed before brushing her lips again. "And I did miss you."

"Come inside and tell me everything," she ordered while tucking her arm through his. "The stock you sent back is wonderful, as always. I've already sold . . . oh, hello, Slade." The moment Jessica turned, she saw him. Quickly, potently, his eyes locked on hers. She had to use all of her strength of will not to draw in her breath. Was there a demand in them? she wondered. A question? Confused, she gave a slight shake of her head. What was it he wanted from her? And why was she ready to give it without even knowing what it was?

"Jessica." There was a faint smile on his face as he waited.

"Michael, this is James Sladerman. He's staying with us for a while and trying to make some order out of the library."

"No small job from what I've seen of it," Michael commented. "I hope you've got plenty of time."

"Enough."

Knowing the housekeeper would be close enough to eavesdrop, Jessica stepped away from Michael and called her. "Betsy, could we have coffee in the parlor? Slade, you'll join us?"

She had expected him to refuse, but he gave her a slow smile. "Sure." He didn't have to look at Michael to see the annoyance before they walked into the parlor.

"Why, Jessica, what's the Queen Anne doing here?"

"Fate," she told him, then laughed as she sat on the sofa. "I'd meant to ask you to find one for me. When I saw it on the shipping list, I wondered if you were psychic."

After studying it for a moment, he nodded. "It certainly suits this room." He sat next to Jessica as Slade settled in an armchair. "No problem with the shipments?"

"No, they're already unpacked. As a matter of fact, three pieces go out tomorrow. David's been ill this past week. Slade helped me get things in order yesterday."

"Really?" Michael took out a wafer-thin gold case, then offered Slade a cigarette. Refusing with a shake of his head, Slade pulled out his own pack. "Do you know antiques, Mr. Sladerman?"

"No." Slade struck a match, watching Michael over the flame. "Unless we count the lesson Jessica gave me yesterday."

Michael sat back, tossing an arm casually over the back of the sofa. "What do you do?" His smooth, neat fingers toyed absently with Jessica's hair. Slade took a hard drag on his cigarette.

"I'm a writer."

"Fascinating. Would I have read any of your work?"

He gave Michael a long, steady stare. "I wouldn't think so."

"Slade is working on a novel," Jessica intervened. There were undercurrents that made her uncomfortable. "You haven't told me yet what it's about."

He caught the look in her eye, recognizing it as a plea for peace. Not yet, he decided. We'll just see what we can stir up. "Smuggling," he said flatly. There was a loud clatter of china from the doorway.

"Damn!" David took a firmer grip on the tray, then gave Jessica a sheepish smile. "I almost dropped the whole works."

"David!" She sprang up to take the coffee tray from him. "You can hardly carry yourself, much less all this." Slade watched him give her a disgruntled look before he flopped into a chair.

David was still pale—or had the loss of color come when smuggling had been mentioned? Slade wondered. There was a faint line of sweat on his brow between his mop of hair and his glasses. After setting down the tray, Jessica turned back to him.

"How do you feel?"

David scowled at her. "Don't fuss."

"All right." She leaned over until her face was level with his. "If I'd known you were going to be such a bad patient, I'd have brought you some crayons and colored paper."

Though he gave her hair a hard tug, he grinned. "Get me some coffee and shut up."

"Oh, yes, sir," she said meekly.

When she turned, David sent Slade a quick wink. "Gotta know how to handle these society types. Hi,

Michael. Welcome back." Reaching in his pocket, he found a crumpled pack of cigarettes. As he searched for matches, his eyes lit on the desk. "Hey, what's this?"

"One of Michael's finds I've already laid claim to," Jessica told him as she brought him his coffee. "You can take care of the paperwork next week."

"Monday," he said firmly, eyeing the desk. "Queen Anne."

"It's lovely, isn't it?" She handed Slade a cup before crossing to it. Opening the lid, she showed off the inside.

Slade felt the back of his neck prickle. There was a rise in tension, he felt it—could nearly smell it. Shifting his eyes from Jessica, he studied both men. Michael added cream to his coffee. David found his match. With a half shrug, Slade told himself he was getting jumpy.

"And wait until you see the rest of the stock," Jessica told David as she came back to the sofa. "Michael outdid himself."

Slade let the conversation hum around him, answering briefly if he was asked a direct question. She was crazy about the kid, he concluded. It showed in the way she teased, lightly bullied, and catered to him. Slade remembered her comment about having wanted a brother or sister. David was obviously her substitute. How far would she go to protect him? he wondered. *All the way* flashed through his mind. If there was one firm impression he'd gotten from Jessica Winslow, it was loyalty.

Her relationship with Michael was less defined. If

they were lovers, Slade concluded that she was very casual about it. Somehow he didn't feel Jessica would be casual about intimacy. Passion, he thought again. There was hot, vibrant passion smoldering in that slender little body. If Michael was her lover, Slade would have seen some sign of it in the kiss they had exchanged at the door.

If she had been in his arms, it would have been there, he thought as his gaze drifted to her mouth. It was soft and unpainted. From ten feet away he could all but taste it. Slowly, irresistibly, desire crept into him, and with it an ache—a dull, throbbing ache he'd never felt before. If he could have her, even once, the ache would go. Slade could almost convince himself of that. He needed to touch that butter-soft skin, experience that promise of passion, then he'd be free of her. He had to be free of her.

Glancing up, Jessica found herself trapped again. His eyes imprisoned her. She could feel herself being pulled—as physical a sensation as if he had taken her hand. She resisted. He's quicksand, her mind flashed. You'll never get away if you take that final step. And yet the risk tempted her.

"Jessica."

Michael took her hand, scattering her thoughts. "Hmm, yes?"

"How about dinner tonight? The little place up the coast you like."

His calm, familiar green eyes smiled at her. Jessica felt her pulses level. This was a man she understood. "I'd love to."

"And don't worry about getting home early,"

David put in. "I'm minding the shop tomorrow; you stay home."

Jessica lifted her brow at the order. "Oh, really?"

David snorted at the dry tone. "There goes Miss Radcliffe," he told Slade. "She forgets I was around when she was twelve and had braces on her teeth."

"How would you like to be flat on your back again?" she invited sweetly. "I'll be ready at seven," she told Michael, ignoring David's grin.

"Fine." Giving her a quick kiss, Michael rose. "See you tomorrow, David. Nice to meet you, Mr. Sladerman."

As he left, Jessica set down her cup and sprang up, as if she had been in one place too long. "I'm going to take Ulysses for a walk on the beach."

"Don't look at me," David drawled. "I have to conserve my energy."

"I wasn't going to ask you. Slade?"

He would have liked to steer clear of her for a while. Resigned, he rose. "Sure. I'll get a jacket."

The beach was long and rocky. From off the bay, the breeze was keen and tinged with salt. Jessica was laughing, stooping to pick up driftwood and toss it for the dog to chase. Ulysses bounded up the beach and back again, running energetic circles around them until Jessica flung another stick. To the right, water hurled itself on rocks, then rose in a misty spray. Slade watched Jessica run to another piece of driftwood.

Doesn't she ever walk? he wondered. She laughed again, holding the stick over her head as the dog leaped clumsily at it. *Don't contact us unless you have something useful.* Slade jammed his hands in his pockets as he remembered his orders. *Watch the woman.* He was watching the woman, damn it. And she was getting to him. Watch what the sunlight does to her hair. Watch how a pair of faded jeans cling to narrow hips. Watch how her mouth curves when she smiles. . . . Watch Detective Sladerman blow everything because he can't keep his mind off a skinny woman with brandy-colored eyes.

"What are you thinking?"

He snapped back to find Jessica a step in front of him searching his face. Cursing himself, he realized he was going to blow more than his cover if he wasn't careful. "That I haven't been to the beach in a long time," he improvised.

Jessica narrowed her eyes. "No, I don't think so," she murmured. "I wonder what it is about you that makes you so secretive." With an impatient gesture, she pushed back her hair. The wind immediately blew it back in her face. "But it's your business, I suppose."

Annoyed, he picked up a rock and hurled it into the breakers. "I wonder what it is about you that makes you so suspicious."

"Curious," she corrected, a bit puzzled by his choice of word. "You're an interesting man, Slade, perhaps because there's so much you don't say."

"What do you want, a biography?"

"You annoy easily," she murmured.

He whirled to her. "Don't push it, Jess."

The nickname pleased her—no one but her father

had ever used it. The fury on his face pleased her too. She'd poked the first hole in his shield. "And if I do?" she challenged.

"You'll get pushed back. I'm not polite."

She laughed. "No, you damn well aren't. Should that scare me?"

She was baiting him. Even knowing it didn't help. Slim and strong, she stood in front of him, her hair whipped around her face by the wind. Her eyes were gold and insolent. No, she wouldn't scare easily. Slade told himself it was to prove a point. Even as he yanked her into his arms, he told himself it was to prove a point. He saw it on her face: anticipation, acceptance. No fear. Cursing her, he brought his mouth down hard on hers.

It was as he thought it would be. Soft, fragrant, pliant. She melted like wax in his arms even as his lips bruised hers. A man could drown in her. The pounding of the surf seemed to echo in his head. There was a sensation of standing in the surf, having it ebb and suck the sand from under him. He dragged her closer.

Her breasts yielded against the hard line of his chest, tempting him to explore their shape with his hands. But all his power, all his concentration, was bound up in the pressure of mouth to mouth. Her hands slid under his jacket, up his back, pressing, urging him to take more. Head swimming, he drew away, struggling to separate himself. With a long, shaky breath, Jessica dropped her head on his shoulder.

"I nearly suffocated."

His arms were still around her. He'd meant to drop

them. Now, with her snuggled close, her hair brushing his cheek, he wasn't certain he could. Then she tilted her face to his—she was smiling.

"You're supposed to breathe through your nose," he told her.

"I think I forgot."

So did I, he mused. "Then take a deep breath," Slade suggested. "I'm not nearly finished yet."

With no less force, with no less turbulence, his mouth returned to hers. This time she was prepared. No longer passive, Jessica made demands of her own. Her lips parted and her tongue met his, searching, teasing, tasting. His flavor was as dark and unsettling as she had imagined. Greedy, she dove deeper. She heard his moan, felt the sudden race of his heart against her own. An urgency filled her so quickly that it took total command. There was nothing but him— his arms, his lips. He was all she wanted.

She had never felt this kind of need or this kind of power. Even when his lips were brutal, she returned the same aggression. Arousal was too tame a word, excitement too bland. Jessica felt a frenzy, a burst of energy that could only be tamed by possession.

Touch me! she wanted to scream as her fingers gripped his hair desperately. Take me! It's never been like this and I can't bear to lose it. She strained against him, her gesture as much a demand as an offering. He was stronger, she knew—the sleek, hard muscles warned her—but his need could be no greater. No need could be greater than the one that throbbed in her, pounded in her. Her body felt assaulted, both helpless and invulnerable.

Oh show me, she thought dizzily. I've waited so long to really know.

A gull screamed overhead. Like a spray of ice water, it jolted Slade back. What the hell was he doing? he demanded as he pushed Jessica away. Or more to the point, what was she doing to him? He'd lost everything—his purpose, his identity, his sanity—in one heady taste of her. Now she stared at him, cheeks flushed with passion, eyes dark with it. Her mouth was moist and swollen from his, parted, with her breath coming rapidly.

"Slade." With his name husky on her lips, she reached for him.

Roughly, he caught her wrist before she could touch him. "You'd better go in."

There was nothing in his eyes now. They were opaque again, unreadable. He stared down at her with a complete lack of interest. For an instant she was too confused to understand. He'd taken her to the edge, to that thin, tenuous border, then had rudely shoved her back as though she hadn't moved him in the least. Shame flooded her face with color. Anger stole in again.

"Damn you," she whispered. Turning, she dashed for the beach steps and took them two at a time.

Jessica dressed with care. There was nothing like the feel of silk against the skin to salve wounded pride. Turning sideways in front of the full-length mirror, she gave a nod of approval. The lines of the dress were simple, except for the surprising plunge in the back that dipped just below the waist. It didn't bother her conscience that she had chosen the dress more with Slade in mind than Michael. And the color suited her mood—a deep, imperial purple. She swept her hair back from her face with two diamond-crusted pins, then let it fall as it chose. Satisfied, Jessica grabbed her evening bag and started downstairs.

She found Slade in the parlor, tightening a screw in a Chippendale commode. His hands were lean and competent. She remembered the feel of them when they'd run over her body in a quick, desperate search. "Well, aren't you handy," Jessica stated.

He glanced up, frowned, and tightened his grip on the screwdriver. Did she have to look like that? he thought darkly. The dress clung everywhere, and from the way she walked by him, he knew she was aware of it. Slade turned the screw savagely. "Betsy complained that the handle was loose," he muttered.

"Jack of all trades," she said lightly. "Drink? I'm fixing martinis."

He started to refuse, then made the mistake of looking over at her. Her back was naked and slim and smooth. The silk shifted enticingly as she reached for a bottle of vermouth. Desire was as breathtaking as a punch in the solar plexus.

"Scotch," he snapped.

She smiled over her shoulder. "Rocks?"

"Straight up."

"Drink like a man, do you, Slade?" Oh, she'd get through that damned indifference, Jessica vowed. And enjoy every minute of it. After pouring him three fingers, she brought the glass to him. He slipped the screwdriver into the back pocket of his jeans and rose. Keeping his eyes on hers, Slade took a long, slow sip of Scotch.

"Dress like a woman, do you, Jess?"

Determined to rattle him, she turned a circle. "Like it?"

"Did you wear it to stir up Adams' juices or mine?" he countered.

With a provocative smile, she turned away to finish the martinis. "Do you think women always dress to stir men up?"

"Don't they?"

"Normally I dress for myself." After pouring a drink, she turned back to regard him over the rim. "Tonight I thought I'd test a theory."

He went to her. The challenge in her eyes and his own ego made it imperative, just as she had anticipated. "What theory?"

Jessica met his angry gaze without faltering. "Do you have any weaknesses, Slade? Any Achilles' heel?"

Deliberately he set down his own glass, then took hers. He felt her stiffen, though she didn't back away. His fingers circled her neck, coaxing her lips to within an inch of his. She felt the warm rush of his breath on her skin.

"You could regret finding out, Jess. I won't treat you like a lady."

She tossed her head back. Though her heart was hammering, she met his eyes with an angry dare. "Who asked you to?"

His fingers tightened; her lashes lowered. The doorbell rang. Slade picked up his drink and downed the rest of it. "Your date," he said shortly, then stalked out of the room.

Slade pulled his car to a halt a short distance away from the restaurant, switched off the engine, pulled out a cigarette, then waited. Michael's Daimler was just being parked by the valet. Slade would have been more comfortable if he could have slipped inside to keep a closer eye on Jessica, but that was too risky.

He saw the car pull up behind him. Tension pricked at the back of his neck as the driver climbed out to approach his car. Slade slipped a hand inside his jacket and gripped the butt of his gun. A badge was pressed against the window glass. Slade relaxed as the man rounded the hood to enter by the passenger side.

"Sladerman." Agent Brewster gave a quick nod of greeting. "You follow the lady, I follow the man. Commissioner Dodson told you I'd be in touch?"

"Yeah."

"Greenhart's looking after Ryce. Not a lot of action there; the guy's been laid up for more than a week. You've got nothing yet, I take it."

"Nothing." Slade shifted to a more comfortable position. "I spent the day at her shop Saturday, helped her uncart a new shipment. If there was anything in it, I'd swear she didn't know it. I had my hands all over everything in that place. She's too damn casual to be hiding anything."

"Maybe." With a weighty sigh, Brewster pulled out a worn black pipe and began to pack it. "If that fancy little shop's the dump site, at least one of 'em's hiding something . . . maybe all three. Seems Ryce is like baby brother. As for Adams . . ." Brewster struck a match and sucked on his pipe. Slade said nothing. "Well, the lady's got the justice's name behind her and a lot of political pressure to keep her name clear, but if she's involved, it's going to hit the fan."

"She's not," he heard himself say, then flipped his cigarette out the window.

"You're in the majority," Brewster commented easily. "Even if she's as pure as a mother's heart, she's in a hell of a spot right now. Pressure's building, Sladerman. The lid's going to blow real soon, and when it does, it's going to get ugly. Winslow might find herself right in the middle. Dodson seems to think you're good enough to keep her out of the way when it goes down."

"I'll take care of her," Slade muttered. "I don't like her being alone with Adams in there."

"Well, I missed my dinner." Brewster touched his rounded stomach. "I'll just go eat on the taxpayers' money and keep an eye on your lady."

"She's not my lady," Slade mumbled.

The restaurant was quiet and candlelit. By the table where Jessica sat with Michael was a breathtaking view of the Sound. On the night-black water there was moonlight and the scattered reflection of stars. The murmur of diners was discreet—low tones, soft laughter. The scent of fresh flowers mixed with the aroma of food and candlewax. Champagne buzzed pleasantly in her head. If someone had told her she'd been working too hard lately, Jessica would have laughed. But now she was completely relaxed for the first time in over a week.

"I'm glad you thought of this, Michael."

He liked the way the light flickered over her face, throwing a mystery of shadows under her cheekbones, enhancing the odd golden hue of her eyes. Why was it she always seemed that much more beautiful when he'd been away from her? And had he, for a dozen foolish reasons, waited too long?

"Jessica." He brought her hand to his lips. "I've missed you."

The gesture and the tone of his voice surprised her. "It's good to have you back, Michael."

Odd that he'd always been known for his smooth lines and was now unable to think how to proceed. "Jessica . . . I want you to start coming with me on the buying trips."

"Come with you?" Her brow creased. "Why, Michael? You're more than capable of handling that end. I hate to admit it, but you're much better at it than I."

"I don't want to be away from you again."

Puzzled, Jessica gave a quick laugh as she squeezed his hand. "Michael, don't tell me you were lonely. I know there's nothing you like better than zipping around Europe hunting up treasures. If you were homesick, it's a first."

His fingers tightened on hers. "I wasn't homesick, Jessica, and there was only one thing I was lonely for. I want you to marry me."

Surprise was a mild term; Jessica was stunned, and her face was transparent. *Marry?* She nearly thought she had misunderstood him. She could hardly conceive of Michael wanting to be married at all, but to her? They'd been together for nearly three years, business associates, friends, but never . . .

"Jessica, you must know how I feel." He placed a

hand over their joined ones. "I've loved you for years."

"Michael, I had no idea. Oh, Michael, that sounds so trite." She ran the fingers of her free hand up and down the stem of her glass. "I don't know what to say to you."

"Say yes."

"Michael, why now? Why all of a sudden?" She stopped the nervous movement of her hand and studied him. "You never even hinted that you had any feelings for me other than affection."

"Do you know how hard it's been," he asked quietly, "contenting myself with that? Jessica, you weren't ready for my feelings. You've been so wrapped up in making a success out of the shop. You needed to make a success of it. And I wanted to build up my own part of it before I asked you. We both needed to be independent."

It was true, all that he said. And yet how was she to suddenly stop seeing him as Michael, her friend, her associate, and see him as Michael, her lover, her husband? "I don't know."

He squeezed her hand, either in reassurance or frustration. "I didn't expect you would so quickly. Will you think about it?"

"Yes, of course I will." And even as she promised, the memory of a violent embrace on a windy beach ran through her mind.

In the late hours the phone rang, but it didn't wake him. He'd been expecting it.

"You've located my property?"

He moistened his lips, then dried them again with

the back of his hand. "Yes . . . Jessica took the desk home. There's a small problem."

"I don't like problems."

Cold beads of sweat broke out on his forehead. "I'll get the diamonds out. It's just that Jessica's always around. There's no way I can take the desk apart and get them while she's in the house. I need some time to convince her to go away for a few days."

"Twenty-four hours."

"But that's not—"

"That's all the time you have . . . or all the time Miss Winslow will have."

Sweat coated his lip and he lifted a trembling hand to wipe it away. "Don't do anything to her. I'll get them."

"For Miss Winslow's sake, be successful. Twenty-four hours," he repeated. "If you don't have them by then, she'll be disposed of. I'll retrieve my property myself."

"No! I'll get them. Don't hurt her. You swore she'd never have to be involved."

"She involved herself. Twenty-four hours."

Chapter 4

JESSICA HAD NO ANSWERS. ALONE, SHE SAT ON THE beach, chin on her knees, and watched the early sun spread streaks of pink above the water. Yards away, Ulysses chased the surf, bounding back to the shore each time it turned on him. He'd given up on the idea of conning Jessica into tossing sticks for him.

She'd always liked the beach at sunrise. It helped her think. The screech of gulls, the pound of water against rock, the burgeoning light, always calmed her mind so that an answer could be found. Not this time. It wasn't as if she'd never considered marriage, sharing a home, raising a family—but she'd never had a clear picture of the man. Could it be Michael?

She enjoyed being with him, talking to him. They shared interests. But . . . oh, there was a *but*, she thought as she lowered her forehead to her knees. An enormous *but*. And he loved her. She'd been blind to it. Where was her sensitivity? she wondered with a surge of guilt and frustration. How could a thing—a business—have been so important that it blocked her vision? Worse, now that she knew, what was she to do about it?

Slade came down the beach steps swearing. How the hell could he keep a rein on a woman who took off before sunrise? Gone walking on the beach, Betsy had told him. Alone on a deserted beach, Slade thought grimly, completely vulnerable to anything and anyone. Did she always have to be moving, doing? Why couldn't she have been the lazy halfwit he'd imagined her to be?

Then he spotted her—head down, shoulders slumped. If it hadn't been for the mass of wheat-colored hair, he would have sworn it was another woman. Jessica stood straight and was always heading somewhere—usually too fast. She didn't curl up in a ball of defeat. Uncomfortable, he thrust his hands in his pockets and walked toward her.

She didn't hear him, but sensed the intrusion and the identity of the intruder almost simultaneously. Slowly she straightened, then looked out at the horizon again.

"Good morning," she said when he stood beside her. "You're up early."

"So are you."

"You worked late. I heard your typewriter."

"Sorry."

"No." A fleeting smile. "I liked it. Is the book going well?"

Slade glanced up as a gull soared over their heads,

white-breasted and silent. "It moved for a while last night." Something's wrong, he thought. He started to sit beside her, then changed his mind and remained standing. "What is it, Jess?"

She didn't answer immediately, but turned her head to study his face. And what would he do, she wondered, if he wanted a woman to marry him? Would he wait patiently, choose the best time, then be satisfied when she asked him to wait for an answer? A ghost of a smile touched her lips. God no.

"Have you had many lovers?" she asked.

"What!"

She didn't pay any attention to his incredulous expression but turned to stare out at the surf again. "I imagine you have," she murmured. "You're a very physical man." The clouds skimming over the water were shot through with red and gold. As she spoke Jessica watched them brighten. "I can count mine on three fingers," she continued in a tone that was more absent than confidential. "The first was in college, a relationship so brief it hardly seems fair to include it. He sent me carnations and read Shelley out loud."

She laughed a little as she settled her chin back on her knees. "Later, when I was touring Europe, there was this older man, French, very sophisticated. I fell like a ton of bricks . . . then I found out he was married and had two children." Shaking her head, Jessica gripped her knees tighter. "After that there was an advertising executive. Oh, he had a way with words. It was right after my father died, and I was . . . groping. He borrowed ten thousand dollars from me and vanished. I haven't been involved with a man since." She brooded out to sea. "I didn't want to get stung again, so I've been careful. Maybe too careful."

He wasn't overly pleased to hear about the men in her life. Forcing himself to be objective, he listened. When she fell silent, Slade dropped down beside her. For the space of a full minute, there was nothing but the sound of crashing waves and calling gulls.

"Jess, why are you telling me this?"

"Maybe because I don't know you. Maybe because it seems I've known you for years." A bit shakily, she laughed and dragged her hands through her hair. "I don't know." Taking a deep breath, she stared straight ahead. "Michael asked me to marry him."

It hit him hard—like a stunning blow to the back of the neck that leaves you disoriented just for an instant before unconsciousness. Very deliberately Slade gathered a handful of sand, then let it sift through his fingers. "And?"

"And I don't know what to do!" She turned to him then, all turbulent eyes and frustration. "I hate not knowing what to do."

Stop it now, he ordered himself. Tell her you're not interested in hearing about her problems. But the words were already slipping out. "How do you feel about him?"

"I depend on Michael," she began, talking fast. "He's part of my life. He's important to me, very important—"

"But you don't love him," Slade finished calmly. "Then you should know what to do."

"It's not that simple," she tossed back. With a sound of exasperation, she started to rise, then made herself sit still. "He's in love with me. I don't want to hurt him, and maybe . . ."

"Maybe you should marry him so he won't be hurt?" Slade gave a mirthless laugh. "Don't be such an idiot."

Anger rose quickly and was as quickly suppressed. It was difficult to argue with logic. More miserable than offended, she watched a gull swoop low over the water. "I know marrying him would only hurt both of us in the long run, especially if his feelings for me are as deep as he thinks they are."

"You're not sure he's in love with you," Slade murmured, considering the other reasons Michael might want her to marry him.

"I'm sure he thinks he is," Jessica returned. "I thought maybe if we became lovers, then—"

"Good God!" He caught her by the shoulder roughly. "Are you considering offering your body as some sort of consolation prize?"

"Don't!" She shut her eyes so she couldn't see the derision in his. "You make it sound so dirty."

"What the hell are you thinking of?" he demanded.

In an uncharacteristic gesture of futility she lifted her hands. "My track record with men has been so poor, I thought . . . well, given a little time he'd change his mind."

"Imbecile," Slade said shortly. "Just tell him no."

"Now you make it sound so easy."

"You're making it complicated, Jess."

"Am I?" For a moment she lowered her forehead to her knees again. His hand was halfway to her hair before he stopped himself. "You're so sure of yourself, Slade. Nothing makes a coward of me more than people I care about. The idea of facing him again, knowing what I have to do, makes me want to run."

He was responding to the fragility she so rarely showed. Deep inside him, something struggled to be free to comfort her. He banked it down an instant before it was too late. "He won't be the first man who's had a proposal turned down."

She sighed. Nothing she'd said had made sense once it had been spoken aloud—everything he said had. Some of the burden lifted. With a half smile, she turned to him. "Have you?"

"Have I what?"

"Had a proposal turned down."

He grinned, pleased that the lost look had left her eyes. "No . . . but then, marriage didn't figure in any of them."

She gave her quick gurgle of laughter. "What did?"

Reaching over, he grabbed a handful of her hair. "Is this color real?"

"That's an abominably rude question."

"One deserves another," he countered.

"If I answer yours will you answer mine?"

"No."

"Then I suppose we'll both have to use our imagination." Jessica laughed again and started to rise, but the hand on her hair stopped her.

The quizzical smile she gave him faded quickly. His eyes were fixed on hers, dark, intense, and for once readable. Desire. Hot, electric, restless desire. And she was drawn to him, already aroused by a look. For the first time she was afraid. He was going to take something from her she wouldn't easily get back, if she managed to get it back at all. He pulled her closer, and she resisted. In an instinctive defense against a nebulous fear, Jessica put her hands to his chest.

"No. This isn't what I want." *Yes, yes, it is,* her eyes told him even while her hands pushed him away.

In one move she was under him on the sand. "I warned you, I wouldn't treat you like a lady."

His mouth lowered, took, and inticed. Fear was buried in an avalanche of passion. At the first taste of him, response overwhelmed her, wild and free. Jessica forgot what she stood to lose and simply experienced. His tongue probed, slowly searching, expertly seducing, while his lips crushed hers in an endless, exquisite demand. She answered, mindlessly willing, desperately wanting. Then he tore his mouth from hers to move over her face, as if to absorb the texture of her skin through the sense of taste alone.

She fretted to have his lips on hers, turning her head in search. Then suddenly, fiercely, he buried his lips at her throat, wrenching a moan from her. The sand made whispering sounds as she shifted, wanting the agonized delight he was causing to go on and on.

Her hands found their way under his sweater, up the planes and muscles of his back, down the hard line of ribs to a lean waist. The moist air smelled of salt and the sea, and faintly, of the musky scent of passion. His mouth found hers again, unerringly, as water crashed like thunder on the rocks nearby. She felt his lips move against hers, though the meaning of his murmur was lost to her. Only the tone—a hint of angry desperation—came through. Then his hands began to search, with bruising meticulousness, from her hips to her breasts, lingering there as if trapped by the softness. She was unaware of the sun beating down on her closed lids, of the coarse sand under her back. There was only his lips and hands now.

Calloused fingers ran over her skin, scraping, kindling fresh fires while feeding those already ablaze. Roughly he caught her bottom lip between his teeth, drawing it into his mouth to suck and nibble until her sighs were moans. In a sudden frenzy Jessica arched against him, center to throbbing center. Denim strained against denim in a thin, frustrating barrier.

On a groan, Slade buried his face in her hair, immersed in the scent of it as he groped for control. But there'd be no control, he knew, with the taste and scent and feel of her overpowering him.

With a muffled oath he rolled from her, springing up before she could touch him and make him forget all reason.

Slade drew air into his lungs harshly, letting it cool the heat that radiated through him. He had to be out of his mind, he thought, to have come that close to taking her. Seconds passed. He could tick them off by the sound of her unsteady breathing behind him. And his own.

"Jess—"

"No, don't say anything. I get the picture." Her voice was thick and wavering. When he turned back, she had risen to brush off the clinging sand. The glint of the morning sun haloed the crown of her head even while the breeze tossed the ends up and back. "You changed your mind. Everyone's entitled." When she started to walk by him, Slade gripped her arm. Jessica jerked against his hold, found it firm, then threw up her chin.

Hurt. Slade could see it all too well beneath the anger in her eyes. It was better that way, he told himself. Smarter. But the words came out of his mouth before he could stop them. "Would you prefer that we'd made love on the beach like a couple of teenagers?"

She'd forgotten where they'd been. Place and time hadn't mattered when the need to love had been paramount. It only cut deeper into her pride that he had remembered and had maintained enough control to stop. "I'd prefer you didn't touch me again," she returned coolly. She lowered her eyes to his restraining hand, then lifted them again, slowly. "Starting now."

Slade's grip only tightened. "I warned you once not to push me."

"Push you?" Jessica retorted. "I didn't start this, I didn't want this."

"No, you didn't start it." He took her shoulders now, giving her three hard shakes. "And I didn't want it either, so back off."

Her teeth snapped together on the final shake. If hurt had outweighed anger before, now the tide was turned. Enraged, Jessica knocked both of his hands away. "Don't you dare shout at me!" she yelled, outdoing him in volume. Behind them water hurled itself against rock, then lifted in a tumultuous spray. "And don't intimate that I've thrown myself at you because I haven't." With her arms pinned, she had to toss her head to free it of blowing hair. Her eyes glinted behind the dancing strands. "I'd have you crawling on your hands and knees if I wanted!"

His eyes became gray slits. Anger mixed with an

uncomfortable certainty that she probably could. "I don't crawl for any woman, much less some snotty little twit who uses perfume as a weapon."

"Snotty little—" She broke off, sputtering. *"Twit!"* she managed after an outraged moment. "Why, you simple-minded, egotistical ass." Unable to think of a better defense, she shoved a hand against his chest. "I hope you haven't put a woman in that novel of yours because you know zip! I'm not even *wearing* any perfume. And I wouldn't need—" Breathing hard, Jessica trailed off. "What the hell are you grinning at?"

"Your face is pink," he told her. "It's cute."

Her eyes flashed, golden fury. The intent for violence was clear in the step she took toward him. Lifting his hands aloft, palms out, Slade stepped back.

"Truce?" He wasn't sure when or how, but sometime during her diatribe his anger had simply vanished. He was almost sorry. Fighting with her was nearly as stimulating as kissing her. Nearly.

Jessica hesitated. Her temper hadn't run its course, but there was something very appealing about the way he smiled at her. It was friendly and a shade admiring. She had the quick notion that it was the first absolutely sincere smile he'd given her. And it was more important than her anger.

"Maybe," she said, not willing to be too forgiving too quickly.

"State your terms."

After a moment's consideration she placed her hands on her hips. "Take back the snotty little twit."

The gleam of pure humor in his eyes pleased her. "For the simple-minded, egotistical ass."

Bargaining was her biggest vice. Jessica curled her fingers and contemplated her nails. "Just the simple-minded. The rest stands."

He hooked his thumbs in the front pockets of his jeans. "You're a tough lady."

"You got it."

When he held out his hand, they shook solemnly. "One more thing." Since they'd dealt with the anger, Slade wanted to deal with the hurt. "I didn't change my mind."

She didn't speak. After a moment he slipped an arm around her shoulders and began to lead her back toward the beach steps. Without too much effort, he blocked out the nagging voice that told him he was making a mistake.

"Slade."

He glanced down at her as they skirted the small grove at the top of the steps. "What?"

"Michael's coming to dinner tonight."

"Okay, I'll stay out of the way."

"No." She spoke too quickly, then bit her lip. "No, actually, I was wondering if you could . . ."

"Play chaperone?" he finished shortly. "Careful, Jess, you're coming close to being a twit again."

Refusing to be angry, she stopped in the center of the lawn and turned to him. "Slade, everything you said on the beach is true. I'd said the same to myself. But I love Michael—almost the same way I love David." When he only frowned at her, she sighed. "What I have to do tonight hurts. I'd just like some moral support. It would be a little easier if you were there during dinner. Afterward I'll handle it."

Reluctant and resigned, Slade let out a long breath.

"Just through dinner. And you're going to owe me one."

Hours later Jessica paced the parlor. Her heels clicked on the hardwood floor, fell silent over the Persian carpet, then clicked again. She was grateful that David had a date. It would have been impossible to have hidden her mood from him, and just as impossible to have confided in him. The business relationship was bound to be strained now between her and Michael. Jessica didn't want to add more problems. Perhaps Michael would even decide to resign. She hated the thought of it.

Oh, it would always be possible to replace a buyer, she thought, but they'd been so close, such a good team. Shutting her eyes, she cursed herself. She couldn't help thinking of Michael in conjunction with the shop. It had always been that way. Maybe if they had known each other before the partnership, like she and David, her feelings would be different. Jessica clasped her hands together again. No, there simply wasn't that . . . spark. If there had been, the shop would never have interfered.

She'd felt the spark once or twice in her life—that quick jolt that says maybe, just maybe. There'd been no spark with Slade, she mused. There'd been an eruption. Annoyed, Jessica shook her head. She shouldn't be thinking of Slade now, or of the two turbulent times she'd been in his arms. It was only right that she concentrate on Michael, on how to say no without hurting him.

Before coming into the room, Slade stopped to watch her. Always moving, he thought, but this time there were nerves beneath the energy. She was wearing a very simple, very sophisticated black dress with her hair caught in a braid over one shoulder. Looking at her, Slade had a moment's sympathy for Michael. It wouldn't be easy to love a woman like that and lose. Unless Michael was a total fool, one glance at her face was going to give him her answer. She'd never have to open her mouth.

"He's going to survive, Jess." When she whirled, Slade strode over to the liquor cabinet. "There are other women, you know." He was deliberately offhand, deliberately cynical, knowing what her reaction would be. Even with his back to her, he thought he could feel the sudden blaze of heat from her eyes.

"I hope you fall hard one day, Slade," Jessica retorted. "And I hope she thumbs her nose at you."

He poured himself a Scotch. "Not a chance," he said lightly. "Want a drink?"

"I'll have some of that." She walked over and snatched the glass from his hand, then took a long sip.

"Dutch courage?" he asked when she swallowed, controlling a grimace.

She gave him a narrow look while the liquor burned her throat. "You're being purposely horrid."

"Yeah. Don't you feel better?"

With a helpless laugh, she shoved the glass back in his hand. "You're a hard man, Slade."

"You're a beautiful woman, Jessica."

The quiet words threw her completely off balance. She'd heard them dozens of times from dozens of people, but they hadn't made the blood hum under her skin. But then, compliments wouldn't roll easily off the tongue of a man like Slade, she thought. And somehow she felt he wasn't only speaking of physical beauty. No, he was a man who'd look beyond what could be seen and into what could only be felt.

Their eyes held, a moment too long for comfort. It occurred to her that she was closer to losing something vital to him now than she had been on the beach that morning.

"You must be a very good writer," she murmured as she stepped away to pour a glass of vermouth.

"Why?"

"You're very frugal with words, and your timing with them is uncanny." Because her back was to him, she allowed herself to moisten her lips nervously. The clock on the mantel gave the melodious chime that signaled the hour. "I don't suppose you'd like to write me a speech before Michael gets here."

"I'll pass, thanks."

"Slade . . ." Hesitating only briefly, Jessica turned to him. "I shouldn't have told you everything I did out on the beach this morning. It really isn't fair to Michael for you to know, and it isn't fair to you that I dropped my life's history on you that way. You're an easy person to confide in because you listen a bit too well."

"Part of my job," he muttered and thought of the endless stream of interviews with suspects, witnesses, victims.

"I'm trying to thank you," Jessica said shortly. "Can't you take it graciously?"

"Don't be grateful until I've done something," he tossed back.

"I'd choke before I'd thank you again." She dumped a splat of vermouth in her glass as the doorbell rang.

Neither man was pleased to be sharing a meal with the other, but they made the best of it. The general conversation eased slowly toward talk of the shop.

"I'm glad you went by for a few hours, Michael." Jessica poked at the shrimp Dijon rather than eating it. "I don't think David's really up to a full day's work yet."

"He seemed well enough. And Mondays are usually slow in any case." He swirled his wine, giving his dinner little more attention than Jessica. "You worry too much, darling."

"You weren't here last week." She shredded a roll into tiny pieces.

Saying nothing, Slade passed her the butter. Glancing down, Jessica saw the mess she'd made and picked up her wine.

"He was well enough today to sell the Connecticut chest to Mrs. Donnigan," Michael commented after noting the exchange.

"David made a sale to Mrs. Donnigan?" Initial surprise turned to humor. "You'd have to know the lady, Slade. She's a died-in-the-wool Yankee who can stretch a dollar like a piece of elastic. Michael sells to her. On a rare occasion I do, but David . . ." Trailing off, she smiled. "How did he manage it?"

"By being very reluctant to part with it. When I came in he was nudging her toward the pecan hope chest, telling her he'd all but promised the other to another customer."

She gave a quick spurt of laughter. "Well, it looks like our boy's learning. I'm going to have to give in and let him go to Europe with you next time."

Briefly, Michael frowned down at his plate, then

very deliberately stabbed a shrimp. "If that's what you want."

Her distress was immediate. Before Jessica could fumble for a new line of conversation, Slade intervened by asking what a Connecticut chest was. She threw him a swift glance of appreciation and let Michael take over.

Why did I say that? she demanded of herself. How could I be insensitive enough to forget that he'd asked me to go to Europe with him the next time? On an inward sigh, Jessica toyed with her dinner. I'm not going to handle this well, she thought. I'm simply not going to handle it well at all.

How different they are. It occurred to her all at once as she watched the two men talk casually. Michael, with his smooth gestures, was well groomed in voice and manner, sleekly dressed. Jessica reflected that she'd never seen him in anything more casual than a polo shirt and golf pants. He was all civilized charm and sophisticated sexuality.

Slade rarely gestured at all. It was as if he knew that body language could give his thoughts away. No, he had a strange capacity for stillness. And she wouldn't term him rugged though he favored jeans and sweaters. Not charming but disarming, she decided. And his sexuality was anything but sophisticated. Animal.

Slade asked questions on antiques when he couldn't have cared less. This would give Jessica a few moments to regain the composure she had so nearly lost. It might also give him the opportunity to form a more concrete opinion of Michael. He seemed harmless enough, Slade reflected. A pretty boy with enough brains to make it his profession. Or enough brains to be one of the rungs on the smuggling ladder. Not the top one, Slade thought instinctively. Not enough guts.

He was the type of man Slade might have matched Jessica with. Polished, intelligent. And he was good looking enough, if you liked that type. Apparently Jessica didn't. They hadn't been lovers. Slade pondered this as he listened to Michael. What sort of man, he wondered, could be around that woman day after day and not make love to her—or go mad? Michael had managed to keep himself in check for nearly three years. Slade calculated that he hadn't been able to do so for as many days. Michael Adams was either madly in love with her or more clever than he looked. Catching the way Michael's eyes would drift to her occasionally, Slade felt a stir of sympathy. Madly in love or not, he wasn't indifferent.

Michael took another sip of wine and tried to continue a conversation he was beginning to detest. He knew Jessica. Oh yes, he thought fatalistically, he knew Jessica. He'd seen her answer in her eyes. The one woman who mattered to him was never going to be his.

All three of them were relieved when Betsy brought in the coffee tray. "Miss Jessica, if you don't start eating more than that, Cook's going to quit again."

"If she didn't quit once a month, she'd throw the entire household off schedule," Jessica said lightly. Food was something she could do without until after she had settled things with Michael.

"I'll just take a cup to the library." Slade was up and pouring his own before Betsy could object. "I've got some things to finish up tonight."

"Fine." Jessica took care not to look at him. "Let's

have ours in the parlor, Michael. No, no, Betsy, I'll carry it," she continued as the housekeeper started to mutter. Slade disappeared before she could lift the tray. "Help yourself to the brandy," she told Michael as they entered the parlor. "I'll just have the coffee."

He poured a generous amount, placing the crystal stopper back in the decanter before turning. Betsy had lit the fire while they were eating. It crackled with a cheer neither Jessica nor Michael were feeling. Remaining across the room, he watched her pour coffee from the china pot into china cups. The set had a delicate pattern of violets on an ivory background. Michael counted each petal before he spoke.

"Jessica." Her fingers tightened on the handle of the creamer and he swore silently. Strange that he'd never wanted her more than at the moment he was sure he'd never have her. He'd been too confident that when the time was right, everything would simply fall into place. "I didn't mean to make you unhappy."

Her eyes lifted to meet his. "Michael—"

"No, you don't have to say anything, it's written all over your face. The one thing you've never been able to do well is hide your feelings." He took a long swallow of brandy. "You're not going to marry me."

Say it quick, she ordered herself. "No, I can't." Rising, she walked over to stand with him. "I wish I felt differently, Michael. I wish I'd known what your feelings were sooner."

He looked into his brandy—the same color as her eyes and just as intoxicating. He set the snifter down. "Would it have made any difference if I'd asked you a year ago? Two years ago?"

"I don't know." Helplessly, she lifted her shoulders. "But as we're basically the same people we were then, I don't think so." She touched his arm, wishing she had better words, kinder words. "I care, Michael, you must know that I do. But I can't give you what you want."

Lifting a hand, he circled the back of her neck. "I can't tell you I won't try to change your mind."

"Michael—"

"No, I'm not going to pressure you now." He gave her neck a gentle squeeze. "But I have the advantage of knowing you well—what you like, what you don't like." Taking her hand, he pressed a kiss in her palm. "I also love you enough not to hound you." With a smile, he released her hand. "I'll see you at the shop tomorrow."

"Yes, all right." Jessica pressed her hands together. She'd felt nothing but regret when he'd pressed his lips to her palm. "Good night, Michael."

When the front door closed behind him, she stood where she was. She had no taste for coffee now, nor the energy to carry the tray to the kitchen and deal with Betsy or the cook. Leaving things as they were, Jessica headed for the stairs.

"Jess?" Slade stopped her with a word. He came down the hall as she paused on the second step. "Okay?"

All of a sudden she wanted badly to cry—to turn, run into his arms, and weep. Instead she snapped at him. "No, it's not okay. Why the hell should it be?"

"You did what you had to do," he said calmly. "He's not going to drive off a cliff."

"What do you know about it?" she tossed back. "You haven't got any feelings. You don't know what it's like to care for someone. You have to have a heart to be hurt." Whirling, she dashed up the stairs, making it almost halfway before she stopped. Shutting her eyes tight, Jessica slammed a fist onto the railing. After a deep breath, she turned and walked back down. He stood at the bottom, waiting.

"I'm sorry."

"Why?" Because her words had cut deeper than he liked, he shrugged. "You were on target."

"No, I wasn't." Wearily, she rubbed a hand over her forehead. "And I haven't any right to use you for a punching bag. You gave me a lot of support today, and I'm grateful."

"Save it," he advised as he turned away.

This time it was her turn to stop him. "Slade." He took two more steps, swore, then turned back to her. His eyes were dark, smolderingly angry, as if her apology had flamed his temper more than her insults. "I realize you might think differently, but you don't go to hell for being kind."

With that, she left him staring after her as she continued up the stairs.

Chapter 5

Two a.m. Jessica heard the old Seth Thomas clock in the hall strike two musical bongs. Her body was exhausted, but her mind refused to settle. Slade's spurts of stop-and-go typing had silenced over an hour before. He could sleep, she thought in disgust as she rolled to her back to stare, again, at the ceiling. But then, he wasn't in an emotional whirl.

Thoughts of Michael drifted to her and she sighed. No, let's be honest, Jessica, she ordered herself. It isn't Michael who's keeping you awake, it's the man two doors down on the left.

Alone in the dark, in the tangle of soft linen sheets, Jessica could feel the scrape of sand against her back, the heat of the sun and bite of the wind on her face. The press of his body against hers. Desire churned in her tired body, awakening pulses she struggled to calm. She felt the ache move slowly from her stomach to her breasts. Quickly she sprang out of bed and tugged on a robe. All she needed was a hot drink to settle her, she decided, almost frantically. If that didn't work, she'd switch on the television until some old movie lulled her to sleep. In the morning she'd have herself in order again. She'd go back to work, stay out of Slade's way until he finished the library and went back to where he came from.

Jessica slipped out of the room and moved on silent bare feet down the hall. She paused in front of Slade's door, even reached for the handle before she caught herself. Good God, what was she thinking of! Moving quickly, she headed for the stairs. Maybe a brandy would be a better idea than the hot drink, she decided.

Out of habit, she went quietly down the steps, avoiding the spots that creaked and groaned. Brandy and an old movie, she told herself. If that didn't put her to sleep, nothing would. Seeing that the parlor doors were closed, she frowned. Now who would have done that? she wondered. They were never closed. With a shrug, she decided Slade had shut them before coming up to write. She crossed the hall and pulled one open.

A light blinded her. It shone straight in her eyes, forcing her to throw up a hand to shield them. Shock came first. She stepped back, stunned by the glare, confused by its source. Before she could speak, Jessica froze. *A flashlight.* No one should be in the closed parlor with a flashlight in the middle of the night. Fear ran coolly over her skin, then lodged like a fist in her throat. Without a second's thought, she turned and raced back up the stairs.

Slade snapped fully awake the moment his door was flung open. A shadow darted toward his bed and instinctively he grabbed it, twisted it, and pinned it underneath him. It gave a quiet whoosh of air as it slammed onto the mattress. At the moment of contact he knew he held Jessica.

"What the hell are you doing?" he demanded as his fingers clamped over her wrists. Her scent flooded his senses; instant desire roughened his voice.

With the wind knocked out of her, Jessica struggled to speak. Fear had her body shuddering under his. "Downstairs," she managed. "Someone's downstairs."

He tensed, but schooled his voice to casualness. "A servant."

"At two o'clock in the morning?" she hissed as anger began to take over. It suddenly seeped into her that he was naked, and that her robe had parted when he had yanked her into bed. Swallowing, she struggled beneath him. "With a flashlight?"

He rolled from her quickly. "Where?"

"The parlor." Snatching her robe together, Jessica tried to pretend that she hadn't been weakened, not for a minute, by desire. She watched his shadow as he tugged on jeans. "You're not going down there?"

"Isn't that what you expected me to do when you came in here?" he countered. He opened a drawer and found his gun.

"No, I didn't think at all. The police." Reaching over, she switched on the light. "We have to call . . ." The sentence died as she saw what he held in his hand. A new bubble of terror rose in her throat. "Where did you get that?"

"Stay here."

He was nearly at the door before Jessica could propel her numb body from the bed. *"No!* You can't go down there with a gun. Slade, how—"

He stopped her with a hard, bruising grip on her shoulder. When they fixed on hers, his eyes were ice cold and expressionless. "Stay put," he ordered, then closed the door firmly in her face.

Too shocked to do otherwise, Jessica stared at the blank wood. What in God's name was going on? she demanded as she pressed her hands to her cheeks. It was crazy. Someone sneaking around the parlor in the middle of the night. Slade handling a big ugly gun as if he'd been born with it in his hand. Nerves jumping, she began to pace the room. It was too quiet, she thought as her fingers laced and unlaced. Just too quiet. She couldn't just stand there.

Slade had just finished a quick, thorough tour of the first floor when the creak of the steps had him whirling. He saw Jessica stagger back against the wall, eyes wide as he turned the gun on her.

"Goddammit!" The word exploded at her as he lowered the gun. "I told you to stay upstairs."

She had enough time to register that she'd seen the stance he'd taken with the gun on a hundred television police shows. Then the trembling started. "I couldn't. Is he gone?"

"Looks that way." Seizing her hand, Slade dragged her into the parlor. "Stay in here. I'm going to check outside."

Jessica sank into a chair and waited. It was dark; the thin, shifting moonlight tossed wavering shadows around the room. Defensively, she curled her feet under her and cupped her elbows with her hands. Fear, she realized, was something she'd rarely dealt with. She wasn't doing a good job of it now. Shutting her eyes a moment, Jessica forced herself to take deep, even breaths.

As the shuddering calmed, her thoughts began to focus. What was a writer doing with a revolver? Why hadn't he called the police? A suspicion rose out of nowhere and she shook it off. No, that was ridiculous. . . . Wasn't it?

When Slade returned to the parlor ten minutes later, she hadn't moved from the chair.

With a flick of the wrist, he hit the switch, flooding the room with light. "Nothing," he said shortly though she hadn't spoken. "There's no sign of anyone, or any sign of a break-in."

"I saw someone," she began indignantly.

"I didn't say you didn't." Then he was gone again, leaving her next retort sputtering on her lips. He came back without the gun. "What did you see?" As he asked he began a more careful search of the room.

Brows drawn together, she watched his practiced movements. "The parlor doors were closed. When I opened them, a light hit my eyes. A flashlight. I didn't see anything."

"Anything out of place in here?"

She continued to watch his deft, professional search as he roamed around the room. No, the suspicion wasn't ridiculous, she realized as her stomach tightened. It was all too pat. He's done this before. He's used that gun before.

"Who are you?"

He heard the chill in her voice as he crouched in

front of the liquor cabinet. None of the crystal had been disturbed. He didn't turn. "You know who I am, Jess."

"You're not a writer."

"Yes, I am."

"What is it?" she asked flatly. "Sergeant? Lieutenant?"

He took the brandy decanter and poured liquor into a snifter. His brain was perfectly cool. He walked to her and held out the glass. "Sergeant. Drink this."

Her eyes stayed level on his. "Go to hell."

With a shrug, Slade set the snifter beside her. A deadly calm washed over her, dulling the sting of betrayal. "I want you out of my house. But before you leave," Jessica said quietly, "I want you to tell me why you came. Uncle Charlie did send you, didn't he? Orders from the commissioner?" The last sentence was full of carefully calculated disgust.

Slade said nothing, debating just how much he'd have to tell her to satisfy her. She was pale, but not with fear now. She was spitting mad.

"Fine." Keeping her eyes on his, she rose. "Then I'll call your commissioner myself. You can pack your typewriter and your gun, Sergeant."

She was going to have to have it all, he decided and wished fleetingly for a cigarette. "Sit down, Jess." When she made no move to obey, he gave her a helpful shove back into the chair. "Just shut up and listen," he suggested as she opened her mouth to yell at him. "Your shop's suspected in connection with a major smuggling operation. It's believed that stolen goods are hidden in some of your imports, then transferred to a contact on this side, probably through the sale of the whole article." She wasn't attempting to speak now, but simply staring at him as if he'd lost his mind. "Interpol wants the head man rather than the few underlings already under observation. He's managed to slip away from them before; they don't want it to happen again. You, your shop, the people who work for you, are under observation until he's in custody or the investigation leads elsewhere. In the meantime the commissioner wants you safe."

"I don't believe a word of it."

But her voice shook. Slade thrust his hands in his pockets. "My information as well as my orders come from the commissioner."

"It's ridiculous." Her voice was stronger now, touched with scorn. "Do you think something like that could go on in my shop without my knowing about it?" Even as she reached for the brandy, she caught the look in his eyes. Jessica's hand froze on the glass, then dropped away. "I see," she said quietly. The pain was dull in her stomach. Briefly, she pressed a hand to it before linking her fingers together. "Did you bring your handcuffs along, Sergeant?"

"Cut it out, Jess." Because he couldn't handle the way she looked at him, Slade turned to prowl the room. "I said the commissioner wanted you protected."

"Was it part of your job to attract me enough so that I might be indiscreet?" When he whirled back, she sprang to her feet to meet his fury with her own. "Is making love to me all in a day's work?"

"I haven't begun to make love to you." Infuriated, he grabbed the lapels of her robe, nearly hauling her off her feet. "And I wouldn't have taken the damn assignment if I'd known you were going to tie me up in knots every time I looked at you. The Bureau thinks you're clean. Don't you understand that only puts you in a more dangerous position?"

"How can I understand anything when I'm not *told* anything?" she tossed back. "What kind of danger could I possibly be in?"

"This isn't a game, Jess." Frustrated, he shook her. "An agent was killed in London last week. He was close, too close, to finding out who's pulling the strings. His last report mentioned a quarter of a million dollars' worth of diamonds."

"What does that have to do with me!" Jessica jerked away from him. "If they think there're diamonds stashed away in one of my imports, let them come in. They can take the furniture apart piece by piece."

"And tip off the number one man," Slade returned.

"How do you know I'm not in charge?" A raging headache was added to the sickness in her stomach. Wearily, Jessica rubbed at her temple. "I run the shop."

He watched her slender fingers knead at the ache. "Not alone."

All movement stopped. Very slowly, Jessica lowered her hand. "David and Michael?" she whispered. Incredulity gave way to anger. "No! I won't have you accusing them."

"No one's accusing anyone yet."

"No, you're here to spy on us."

"I don't like it any better than you."

"Then why are you here?"

The deliberate scorn in her tone made him want to

strangle her. He spoke slowly, brutally. "Because the commissioner didn't want his goddaughter to end up with her beautiful throat slit."

Her color drained at that, but she kept her eyes level. "Who would hurt me—David, Michael? Even you must see how absurd that is."

"You'd be surprised what people do to survive," he said tersely. "In any case, there are other people involved—the kind who wouldn't think of you as any more than an expendable obstacle."

She didn't want to think about that—couldn't if she wanted to stop herself from having a bout of hysteria. Be practical, she ordered herself. Be logical. This time she lifted the brandy and drank deeply before speaking. "If you're with the NYPD you have no jurisdiction here."

"The commissioner has a lot of clout." The hint of color that seeped back into her cheeks relieved him. She was tougher than she looked. "In any case I'm not here about the smuggling, not officially."

"Why are you here—officially?"

"To keep you out of trouble."

"Uncle Charlie should have told me."

Slade lifted his shoulders in a half shrug as he looked around the room. "Yeah, maybe. There's no way of telling if he was after something in here, or slipping through this room to another. Not with the way this house is set up." With a frown, he ran a hand absently over his bare chest. "Do you see anything out of place in here?"

Jessica followed the sweep of his eyes. "No. I don't think he could have been around very long. You didn't stop typing until one. Wouldn't it make sense for him to wait until all the lights were out before he broke in?"

He started to remind her that no one had broken in, then changed his mind. If it helped her to believe it had been a stranger, she might sleep better. He thought of David, who had a room on the east wing of the first floor. "I've got to call in my report. Go on to bed."

"No." Unwilling to admit that she couldn't bring herself to go upstairs alone, Jessica lifted the brandy again. "I'll wait."

She sat as he went out to the phone in the hall. Purposely, she tuned out his conversation, though it was carried on in such quiet tones that she would have had to strain to hear. Her shop, she thought. How was it possible for her shop to be tangled up in something as fantastic as international smuggling? If it hadn't been so frightening, she would have laughed.

Michael and David. With a brisk shake of her head, she shut her eyes. No, that part she wouldn't believe. There was a mistake somewhere, and in time the police or the FBI or whoever was haunting her would realize it.

A burglar had been in the parlor. It was as simple as that. Hadn't Betsy grumbled a dozen times about her not using the alarm system? The image of Slade with the gun in his hand came back to her too clearly. That was something she couldn't shut out.

When he came back into the room, Jessica was sitting very still, eyes closed. There were shadows under them. What he'd just learned on the phone wasn't going to make them go away, but perhaps a good night's sleep would.

"Come on," he said briskly, trying not to soften as her eyes shot open in alarm at his voice. "You're tired. Go up and take a pill if you can't sleep. And you're not going in to the shop tomorrow."

"But I have to," she began.

"You have to do as you're told from here on," he corrected. "You'll be safer here where I can keep an eye on you. Starting now, you don't leave the house without me. Don't argue." Taking her hand, he hauled her to her feet. "You haven't got any choice at this point; you have to trust me."

She did. Jessica realized as he pulled her up the steps that if everything else was a maze of confusion, that was clear. That very quick first impression she'd gotten when she'd all but run into him at the bottom of the staircase had been viable. With him she was safe.

"I don't like knowing you're a cop," she murmured.

"Yeah, I'm not always crazy about it myself. Go to bed, Jess." He dropped her arm as they came to her door. Before he could move on, Jessica grabbed his hand.

"Slade . . ." She hated what she was going to ask, hated admitting to herself, much less him, that she was terrified of being alone. "I . . ." She looked away from the impatience in his eyes and glanced into her darkened room. "Could you stay?"

"I told you, I've got my orders from the commissioner."

"No, I don't mean . . ." She moistened her lips. "I mean with me—tonight."

She looked up at him, pale, soft, vulnerable. He felt the blood start to pound in his chest. In defense, his voice was blunt and cold. "When I go to bed with a woman, I tend to give her my complete attention. I haven't got time for that now."

She felt a flutter that was both panic and excitement. "I'm not asking you to make love with me, just not to leave me alone."

He allowed his eyes to rake down her. Warm flesh, soft curves, and ice-blue silk. "Do you think I'd spend the night with you and not have you?"

"No." The answer came quick and quiet. The flutter became a throb.

In a quick move calculated to frighten her, Slade backed her up against the door. "You haven't the experience to deal with me, lady." Not quite gently, his hand closed over her throat. Beneath his palm he felt the wild scramble of her pulse, but her eyes . . . her eyes were tawny and unafraid. He wanted her with a desperation that threatened to drive everything else aside. "I'm not one of your polite country club men, Jess," he told her in a dangerously quiet voice. "You don't know the places I've been, the things I've done. I could show you tricks that would make your French lover look like a Boy Scout. If I decided I wanted you, you couldn't run fast enough."

She could barely hear him over the dull thud of her heart. Her eyes had misted over with desire. "Which of us is running, Slade?" Her arms were already heavy, but she lifted them. In one long slow stroke, she ran her hands up his naked back. He stiffened. The fingers on her throat tightened swiftly. She pressed her body to his.

"Damn you, Jess." On a groan, his mouth came down to savage hers.

Her senses whirled from the onslaught, but she clung. This was what she wanted—the mindless passion he could bring her on the instant of contact. The kiss wasn't loverlike; it wasn't the worshipful merging of lips, the gentle teasing of tongues. It was madness. Jessica abdicated her sanity without a second thought. Let him teach her what he would.

He ripped the robe from her where they stood, then gave into the driving need to let his hands mold every inch of her. Softer, inconceivably softer than he imagined, her skin seemed to flow under his fingers. Within seconds he had her trembling, one wracking, convulsive shudder after another. Her thighs were slim and strong. Running a hand up them, he found her, then took her gasping to a staggering peak until she swayed helplessly in his arms.

Slade swore again, knowing he couldn't stop. He had told himself he would treat her callously and then walk away—to save her . . . to save himself. Now she was moist and warm and pliant in his arms. Her fragrance clung to the air, seducing him. He shook his head, struggling to clear it, but she pressed her lips to his throat, huskily murmuring his name.

He was with her in bed, not even aware if he had dragged or carried her there.

Jessica twisted under him, answering his kiss deliriously as his hands moved everywhere. He gave her no chance to orient herself. There was a tangle of sheets under her, the soft fabric of his jeans against her legs, but she was only aware of the hurricane. That's where he took her—all speeding wind and black sky. His ragged breathing shivered into her ear before his tongue darted inside.

In a zigzagging journey that had her mind spinning, he ran open-mouthed, nibbling kisses down her throat to the hollow between her breasts. She arched, her nipples hard with need, but he continued down and ran his tongue along the line of her ribs. Half mad, she dug her fingers into his hair, wanting him to take her before she exploded, wanting the agonizing pleasure to go on forever.

Greedily, he came back to her breast, the moist trail his tongue left causing her to shudder with fire and ice by turns. His teeth nipped into the soft swell of flesh while with a fingertip he began a slow, torturous path around the other. Lips and finger circled in until she was writhing beneath him. He drew her nipple into his mouth, catching the other arching point between his thumb and finger. Jessica cried out as the dual pleasure exploded, then was lost in wave after wave of sensation as his teasing became rampant hunger.

She was tugging at his jeans, but he shifted away from her seeking hands. Without the restriction he knew he'd take her instantly. He was far from ready. He'd sensed her passion, knew it lay smoldering, but now it was engulfing him in a heat he hadn't foreseen. She was wildly responsive, like a thoroughbred mare given her head. He wanted to drive her—drive them both—to the breaking point.

The musky, woodsy scent seemed to emanate from her skin wherever he buried his lips. Her body was slender, almost too slender, but with a seductive womanly softness that made him want to go on touching and tasting until there was no inch of her he didn't know. When his mouth brushed low over her stomach, she moaned, nails digging into his shoulders as she urged him down. He could hear his name trembling out of her lips between raw, gasping breaths. But when his tongue sought and found the center of her pleasure, he lost everything else.

He drove her to peak after peak. Exhausted, Jessica hungered for more. Her skin was fused to his, both hot and damp with desire. Her body was stunningly alive, throbbing from thousands of minute pulses he had discovered and exploited. Even his name wouldn't form on her lips any longer. Together they struggled with the last barrier of clothing that kept them apart. She found his hips, lean and long-boned; his thighs, firm and muscled.

They came together savagely, each gasping from the shock of power.

She couldn't stop the shudders. They continued to race through her long after Slade lay beside her, silent. Her body ached. And glowed. Did we make love or war? Jessica wondered dizzily. Whatever had happened between them had never happened to her before, and she knew with a certainty that it would never happen with any other man.

None of her inhibitions had surfaced—he wouldn't have allowed them to. Was there another man with his strength, his intensity, his . . . savagery? Not for her, Jessica realized, instinctively rolling to him. There had never been, nor would there ever be anyone else for her. She'd lost that vital part of herself to him long before they had ever gone to bed—her heart.

Oh, I love you, she thought, whoever, whatever you are. And the surest way to turn you away from me now is to tell you. Closing her eyes, Jessica rested her head on his shoulder. You're already wondering how you lost control enough to take me to bed, she concluded with instinctive accuracy. Already wondering how to prevent this from happening again. *But I'm not going to lose you.* The vow formed firmly as she ran a hand over his chest. You're not getting away, Slade; struggle all you want. Lightly, she ran a trail of kisses over his shoulder to his throat.

"Jess." Slade put up a hand to stop her. He'd never be able to think clearly with her touching him. If he was going to find his way out of the quicksand he was rapidly sinking in, he had to think.

Jessica merely kissed the fingers that got in her way, then trailed her lips to his cheek. "Hold me," she murmured. "I want your arms around me."

With an effort, Slade resisted the husky demand and the soft lips that insisted on clouding his brain. "Jessica, this isn't smart. We've got—"

"I don't want to be smart, Slade," she interrupted. She shifted so that her head was just above his, her lips just above his. "Don't talk, not tonight." When her fingers ran down his side, she had the satisfaction of feeling his quick, involuntary tremor. "I want you." Her tongue traced his lips. She felt the sudden thunder of his heart against her breast. "You want me. That's all there is tonight."

In the darkness he could see the pale clouds of hair, the moonlit skin shadowed by the slash of cheekbone. He saw the amber fire of her eyes before her mouth took his and captured him.

Chapter 6

SLADE WOKE BESIDE HER. SHE WAS DEEP IN AN EX-hausted sleep, her breathing slow and regular. There were shadows under the sweep of lashes, dark smudges against pale skin. His arm was around her slim waist; in sleep he'd betrayed himself by wanting her close. They shared the same pillow. He spent several minutes cursing himself before he rolled out of bed. Jessica didn't even stir. He grabbed up his jeans and went to his own room and straight to the shower.

Deliberately, Slade turned the cold on full. Hadn't he saturated himself enough with her last night? he asked himself furiously as the icy spray hit his body like sharp pinpricks. Did he have to wake up wanting her? Need for her, this kind of consuming need, was going to interfere with his job. Slade had to remind himself again and again that Jessica was a job, only a job.

And in the brief phone conversation the night before, he had been told enough to make him realize that her position had become only more delicate. Someone wanted something in her house—someone she trusted. Knowing who it was wouldn't be enough. Slade had to find out what it was. Or rather the Feds had to find out what, he corrected grimly. He had to stick to her like glue until it was all over.

Why the hell don't they let me get her out of here? he thought on a fresh burst of fury. The order over the phone had been firm and unarguable. Jessica stayed. The investigation couldn't be jeopardized by letting her walk. She stayed, Slade repeated silently. And he wasn't to let her out of his sight for the next forty-eight hours. That didn't include sleeping with her, he reminded himself as he let the cold water sluice over his head. It didn't include getting so caught up in her that he forgot what he was doing there in the first place. And how the hell was he supposed to live in the same house with her now and not touch her?

He grabbed the soap and lathered himself roughly. Maybe it would wash away the woodsy scent that seemed to have crept into his own skin.

Waking, Jessica reached for him. He was gone, and so, instantly, was her peace. The few hours of sleep had left her tightly strung instead of relaxed. If he had been there, if she could have turned to him on wakening, she wouldn't have felt the sick sense of loss.

David and Michael. No, she couldn't even allow herself to think it. Covering her face with her hands,

Jessica struggled to block it out. But then she could see the icy look in Slade's eyes when he had aimed the gun on her. It's madness, it's a mistake. A quarter of a million in diamonds. Interpol. *David and Michael.*

Unable to bear it, she sprang out of bed. She needed to clear her brain, to think. The house felt like an airless prison. She threw on her clothes and headed for the beach.

When he came by her room to check on her ten minutes later, Slade found the bed empty. The quick panic was as uncharacteristic as it was unprofessional. Hurriedly, he checked the bath and her sitting room before going downstairs. He didn't find Jessica in the dining room, but Betsy.

"Where is she?" he demanded.

Betsy cleared off the place she had set for Jessica, then scowled at him. "So you're in a chipper mood too."

"Where's Jessica?"

Betsy sent him a shrewd look. "Looks sick this morning, wonder if she caught David's flu. Down at the beach," she continued before he could snap at her.

"Alone?"

"Yes, alone. Didn't even take that overgrown mutt with her. Said she's not going into work today, and . . ." Betsy placed her hands on her hips and scowled at his retreating back. "Well," she muttered and clucked her tongue.

It was cold. Concealing his shoulder holster under his jacket was simple. By the time Slade had reached the beach steps, he'd nearly run out of curses. Hadn't anything he'd said to her the night before gotten through? He spotted her standing near the breakers and tore down the steps and across the sand.

Jessica heard his approach and turned. Whatever she might have said slipped back down her throat as he grabbed her by the shoulders and shook her.

"You idiot! What are you doing down here alone? Don't you know the position you're in?"

Her hand swung out, connecting sharply with his cheek. The slap stunned both of them, causing angry eyes to meet angry eyes in quick surprise. His grip loosened enough for Jessica to step back. "Don't you shout at me," she ordered, automatically soothing the flesh his hands had bruised. "I don't have to take that from anyone."

"You'll take it from me," he said evenly. "I'll give you that one, Jess, but remember, I hit back. What are you doing out here?"

"I'm taking a walk," she snapped. "I arranged for David to take over the shop today, as per your orders, Sergeant."

So we're back to that, he reflected and dug his hands into his pockets. His hair whipped unheeded around his face. "Fine. My next order is that you're not to leave the house until I say so."

The fire in her eyes was suddenly misted with tears. Hugging herself, she spun away from him. She'd show him anger, she'd show him passion, but she refused to show him weakness. "House arrest?" she said thickly.

He'd rather have had her slap him again than cry. "Protective custody," he countered. With a sigh, he placed his hands on her shoulders. "Jess . . ."

Swiftly she shook her head, knowing that kind words would undermine her completely. When she felt his brow drop to the top of her head, she squeezed her eyes tight.

"Don't fall apart now," he murmured. "It won't be for very long. When it's over—"

"When it's over, what?" she interrupted in swift despair. "Will one of the people closest to me be in jail? Am I supposed to look forward to that?" On a long breath, she opened her eyes and looked out to sea. The water was choppy, white-capped and gray. A storm was coming in, she thought dispassionately. The sky was beginning to boil with it.

"You're supposed to get through today," he told her, tightening his grip. "Then you're supposed to get through tomorrow."

Life, she mused. Is that really how life's supposed to be? Is that how he felt about his? "Why did you leave me alone this morning?"

His hands dropped away from her shoulders. Without turning, Jessica knew he'd stepped back. Gathering her courage, she faced him. All the guards were back. If her body had not still ached from the fury of lovemaking, she might have thought she'd imagined all of the night before. The man staring at her showed no hint of emotion.

"You're going to tell me it was a mistake," she managed after a moment. "Something that shouldn't have happened and won't happen again." Her chin came up as love warred with pride. "Please don't bother."

He should have let her go. He intended to let her

go. Before he could stop himself, Slade took her arm, carefully wrapping his fingers around it as if measuring its size and strength. "I'm going to tell you it was a mistake," he said slowly. "Something that shouldn't have happened. But I can't tell you it won't happen again. I can't be near you and not want you."

The man shifted his position in the cover of trees. With businesslike movements, he opened the briefcase and began to fit the pieces of the rifle together. For the moment he paid little attention to the two figures down on the beach. One thing at a time. That was one of the reasons for his success in his field. He'd only had the contract for four hours and was relatively pleased that it would take him little more than that to complete it.

After snapping on the sight, he pulled out a handkerchief. The brisk wind wasn't doing his head cold any good. But then, ten thousand dollars bought a lot of antihistamines. After sneezing softly, he replaced his handkerchief, then drew a bead on the figures on the beach.

Jessica felt some of her strength returning. "Why was it a mistake then?"

Slade let out an impatient breath. *Because I'm a cop from the Lower East Side who's seen things I could never tell you about. Because I want you so much—not just now, this minute, but tomorrow, twenty years from now—and that scares me.*

"Oil and water, Jess, it's as simple as that. You wanted to walk, we'll walk." Slipping his hand from her arm, he interlaced his fingers with hers, then turned away from the shore.

He lowered his rifle as Slade blocked his clear shot of Jessica. The contract was for the woman only, and business was business. The wind fluttered at his drab-colored overcoat and snuck underneath it. Sniffling, he brought his handkerchief out again, then settled down to wait.

Jessica kicked a pebble into a clump of rocks. "You are a writer, aren't you?"

"So I tell myself."

"Then why do you do this? You don't like it—it shows."

It wasn't supposed to show. The fact that she could see what he'd successfully concealed from everyone—including himself from time to time—infuriated Slade. "Look, I do what I have to, what I know. Not everybody has a choice."

"No," she disagreed. "Everyone has a choice."

"I've got a mother waiting tables and living off a dead cop's pension." The words exploded from him, stopping her. "I've got a sister in her third year of college who's got a chance to be something. You don't pay tuition with rejection slips."

Jessica lifted both hands to his face. Her palms were cool and soft. "Then you made your choice, Slade. Not every man would have made the same one. When the time comes, and you publish, you'll have everything."

"Jess." He took her wrists, but held them a moment

instead of pulling her hands from his face. Her pulse speeded instantly at his touch, drawing an unwilling response from him. "You get to me," he muttered.

"And you don't like it." She leaned toward him, lashes lowering.

He crushed her to him, devouring the willing mouth. It was as cool as her hands but heated quickly beneath his. Already frantic, he grabbed her hair, drawing her head back farther so he could plunder all the sweet, moist recesses. Her arms went around his neck, imprisoning him in the softness, the fragrance, the need.

The back of his head was caught in the crosshairs of the scope of a high-powered rifle with a sophisticated silencer.

"Jess." His lips moved against hers with the sound of her name. He broke away only to catch her close to his chest, holding her there while he tried to steady himself. "You're tired," he said when he heard her sigh. "We'll go in. You should get some more sleep."

She allowed him to shift her to his side. Patience, she told herself. This isn't a man who gives himself easily. "I'm not tired," she lied, matching her steps to his. "Why don't I give you a hand in the library?"

"That's all I need," he muttered, casting his eyes up. In his peripheral vision, he caught a quick flutter of white among the thinning leaves in the grove. He tensed, muscles tightening as he strained to see. There was nothing more than a rustling, easily caused by the wind. Then the flutter of white again.

"I'm terrific at organizing if I put my mind to it," Jessica claimed as she stepped in front of him. "And I—" The breath was knocked out of her as Slade shoved her to the ground in back of a small outcropping of rock. She heard a quick ping, as if stone had struck stone. Before she could fill her lungs with air, he'd drawn out his gun. "What is it? What's wrong?"

"Don't move." He didn't even look at her, but kept her pinned beneath him as his eyes swept the beach. Jessica's eyes were locked on his gun.

"Slade?"

"He's in the grove, about ten feet to the right of where we are now," he calculated, thinking out loud. "It's a good position; he won't move—at least for a while."

"Who?" she demanded. "What are you talking about?"

He brought his eyes to hers briefly, chilling her with the hard, cold look she'd seen before. "The man who just took a shot at you."

She went as still and stiff as a statue. "No one did, I didn't hear—"

"He's got it silenced." Slade shifted just enough to get a clearer view of the beach steps. "He's a pro, he'll wait us out."

Jessica remembered the odd sound she'd heard just as Slade had shoved her to the ground. Stone hitting stone. Bullet hitting rock. A wave of dizziness swept over her, clouding her vision until she saw nothing but a gray mist. From a distance she heard Slade's voice and struggled against the faintness. Heart pounding in her ears, she focused on him again. He was still looking beyond her to the beach steps.

". . . that we know he's there."

"What?"

Impatiently, Slade looked down at her. There

wasn't a trace of color in her face. Against the pallor, her eyes were dull and unfocused. He couldn't allow her the luxury of going into shock. "Snap out of it and listen to me," he said harshly, catching her face in his hand. "Odds are he doesn't know we've made him. He probably thinks we're back here making love. If my cover was blown, he'd have taken care of me instead of waiting to get a clear shot at you. Now you've only got to do one thing, Jess, understand?"

"One thing," she repeated with a nod.

"Stay put."

She nearly gave way to a hysterical giggle. "That sounds like a good idea. How long do you think we'll have to stay here?"

"You stay until I get back."

Her arms came around him quickly and with desperate strength. "You're not going out there! He'll kill you."

"It's you he wants," Slade said flatly as he pried her arms away from his neck. "I want you to do exactly as I say."

He wriggled on top of her and managed to shrug out of his jacket, then the shoulder holster. After tugging his shirt out of his jeans, he tucked the gun in the back waistband. "I'm going to stand up, and after a minute I'll walk over to the steps. He'll either think you wouldn't play games or that we're finished and you're staying out for a while."

She didn't hold on to him because she knew it was useless. He was going to do it his own way. "What if he shoots you?" she asked dully. "A hell of a body-guard you'd make dead."

"If he's going to, he'll do it the minute I stand up,"

Slade told her, cupping her face again. "Then you'll still have the gun, won't you?" He kissed her, hard and quick, before she could speak. "Stay put, Jess. I'll be back."

He rose nonchalantly, still looking down at her. Jessica counted ten long, silent seconds. Everything in her system seemed to be on slow motion. Her brain, her heart, her lungs. If she breathed at all, she was unaware of it. She lay in a vacuum of fear. Slade grinned at her, a flash of reassurance that didn't reach his eyes. Numbly she wondered if the smile was for her benefit or for the man in the grove.

"No matter what, you stay where you are." With this he turned away from her and strolled easily to the beach steps. He hooked his thumbs lazily in his pockets as if every muscle in his body weren't tensed, waiting. A thin stream of sweat rolled down his back.

A hell of a bodyguard you'd make dead. Jessica's words played back to him as he forced himself to take the steps slowly. He knew how close that one silent bullet had come. He was taking a chance coming out in the open, not only with himself, but with Jessica.

Calculated risk, Slade reminded himself. Sometimes you played the odds. He counted the steps off. Five, six, seven. . . . It wasn't likely the gunman had the rifle trained on him now. He'd be waiting for Jessica to make a move from behind the clump of rocks. Ten, eleven, twelve. . . . Did she listen this time? he thought with a quick flash of panic. Don't look back. For God's sake don't look back. There was only one way left to keep her safe.

The moment he reached the top, Slade drew out his gun and dashed for the trees.

The carpet of dried leaves would betray him. Slade counted it a mixed blessing. It would distract the man's mind from Jessica. He took a zigzagging pattern toward the place where he had spotted the flutter of white. Just as he dashed behind an oak, he heard the dull thud. Dispassionately he saw splinters of bark fly out, inches from his shoulder.

Close, he thought. Very close. But his brain was cool now. The man would know he'd botched the contract. Just as he'd know, if Slade's luck ran out, that the police were involved. Slade's gun and his shield would tell the pro all he needed to know.

Patiently, Slade waited. Five eternal minutes became ten. The sweat was drying cold on his back. Neither man could move soundlessly, so neither moved at all, one laying seige to the other. A bird, frightened off by Slade's mad rush into the grove, came back to settle on a limb and sing joyfully. A squirrel hunted acorns not ten feet away from where he stood. Slade didn't think at all, but waited. The storm-brewing clouds closed in, completely blocking out the sun. Now the grove was cold and gloomy. Wind whipped through his loose shirt.

There was a muffled sneeze and a rustle of leaves. Instantly Slade sprang out toward the sound, hitting the ground and rolling when he caught a quick glimpse of the man and the rifle. Prone, he fired three times.

Jessica lay numbed by a fear icier than the wind off the Sound. That was all she could hear—the wind and the water. Once she had loved the sound of it, the howling wind, the passionate crash of water against rock. Staring up at the sky, she watched the clouds boil. With one hand she clutched Slade's discarded jacket. The leather was smooth and cold, but she could just smell him. She concentrated on that. If she could smell him, he was alive. If she willed it hard enough for long enough, he'd stay alive.

Too long! her mind shouted. It's been too long! Her fingers tightened on the leather. He'd said he'd be back. She was going to believe that. With her fingertips, she touched her lips and found them cold. The warmth he'd left there had long since faded.

I should have told him I love him, she thought desperately. I should have told him before he left. What if. . . . No, she wouldn't let herself think it. He was coming back. Painfully, she shifted enough so that she could watch the beach steps.

She heard the three rapid shots and froze. The pain in her chest snapped her out of it. Her lungs were screaming for air. Dimly, Jessica ordered herself to breathe before she scrambled up and ran. Fear made her clumsy. Twice she stumbled on her way up the steps, only to haul herself up and force more speed into her legs. She broke into the grove, skidding on cracked leaves and branches.

Slade sprang around the moment he heard her. He was quick, but not quick enough to prevent her from seeing what he'd been determined she wouldn't see. Jessica stopped her headlong rush into his arms, relief turning to shock and shock to trembling.

Cursing, he stepped in front of her, blocking her view. "Don't you ever listen?" he demanded, then pulled her into his arms.

"Is he . . . did you . . ." Unable to finish, she shut

her eyes. She wouldn't be sick, she ordered herself. She wouldn't faint. One of his shirt buttons ground into her cheek and she concentrated on the pain. "You're not hurt?"

"No," he said shortly. This aspect of his life should never have touched her, he berated himself. He should have seen to it. "Why didn't you stay on the beach?"

"I heard the shots. I thought he'd killed you."

"Then you'd have done us both a lot of good rushing in here." He pulled her away, took one look at her face, and yanked her back into his arms. "It's all right now."

For the first time his tone was gentle, loving. It broke her down as his shouting and anger would never have done. She began to weep in raw, harsh sobs, the fingers of one hand digging into his shirt, the fingers of the other still holding his jacket.

Without a word he led her to the edge of the grove. He sat on the grass, then drew her down into his lap and let her cry it out. Not knowing what else to do, he rocked, stroked, and murmured.

"I'm sorry," she managed, still weeping. "I can't stop."

"Get it all out, Jess." His lips brushed her hot temple. "You don't have to be strong this time."

Burying her face against his chest, she let the tears come until she was empty. Even when she quieted, he stroked the hair from her damp face, rocking her with a gentle rhythm. The need to protect had long since stopped being professional. If he could have found the way, Slade would have blocked the morning from her mind—taken her away somewhere, someplace where no ugliness could touch her.

"I couldn't stay on the beach when I heard the shots."

"No." He kissed her hair. "I suppose not."

"I thought you were dead."

"Ssh." He took her lips this time with a tenderness neither of them had known he possessed. "You should have more faith in the good guys."

She wanted to smile for him but threw her arms around his neck instead. The contact was another reassurance that he was whole and safe. "Oh, Slade. I'm not sure I could live through something like that again. *Why?* Why would anyone want to kill me? It just doesn't make sense."

He drew her away so that their eyes met. Hers were red and swollen from weeping, his cool and direct. "Maybe you know something and don't even realize it. The pressure's on, and whoever's in charge of this business is smart enough to know it. You've become a liability."

"But I don't *know* anything!" she insisted, pressing the heels of her hands to her temples. "Someone wants to kill me and I don't even know who it is or why. You said that . . . that man was a professional. Someone paid him to kill me."

"Let's go inside." He pulled her to her feet, but she jerked away. The helpless weeping was over and the strength was back, though it had the dangerous edge of hysteria.

"How much was I worth?" she demanded.

"That's enough, Jess." He took her by the shoulders for one quick shake. "Enough. You're going to go in and pack a bag. I'll take you to New York."

"I'm not going anywhere."

"The hell you aren't," he muttered as he started to pull her toward the house.

Jessica yanked out of his grip for the second time. "You listen to me. It's *my* life, my shop, my friends. I'm staying right here until it's over. I'll do what you tell me to a point, Slade, but I won't run."

He measured her slowly. "I've got to call this business in. You're to go straight to your room and wait for me."

She nodded, not trusting his easy acceptance. "All right."

He nodded, not trusting hers.

The moment she stepped into her room, Jessica began to peel off her clothes. It was suddenly of paramount importance that she scrub off every grain of sand, every lingering trace of the time she had spent on the beach. She turned the hot water in the tub on full until the room was misted with steam. Plunging in, she gasped at the shock of the heat against her chilled skin, but took the soap and lathered again and again until she could no longer smell the scent of salt water—the scent of her own fear.

It had been a nightmare, she told herself. This was normalcy. The cool green tile on the walls, the leafy fern at the window, the ivory towels with the pale green border she had chosen herself only the month before.

A month ago, she thought, when her life had been

simple. There'd been no man then coolly attempting to kill her for a fee. David had still been the brother she'd never had. Michael had been her friend, her partner. She hadn't even heard of a man named James Sladerman.

She closed her eyes, and pressed hot, damp fingers to them. No, it wasn't a nightmare. It was real. She had lain curled behind a pile of rocks while a man she barely knew—and loved—had risked his life to protect hers. It was horribly, horribly real. And she had to face it. The time was over when she could try to pass off what Slade had told her as a mistake. While she had been blindly trusting, someone she loved had deceived her, involved her. Used her.

Which one? she asked herself. Which one could she believe it of? Would either David or Michael have stood passively by while someone arranged to have her killed? Lowering her hands, Jessica forced herself to be calm. No, whatever else she would believe, she wouldn't believe that.

Slade thought she might know something without being aware of it. If that was true, she was no closer to the solution than she had been before. Jessica slid her body down in the tub and closed her eyes again. There was nothing for her to do but wait.

Anything but satisfied with his conversation with his contact, Slade put a call through directly to the commissioner.

"Sergeant, what have you got for me?"

"Someone tried to kill Jessica this morning," he answered curtly.

For a moment there was dead silence on the wire. "Give me the details," Dodson demanded.

Briefly, emotionlessly, Slade reported while his knuckles turned white on the receiver. "She won't leave voluntarily," he finished. "I want her out, today. Now. I need you to officially give me the right to put her in protective custody. I can have her in New York in less than two hours."

"I take it you've already checked in with this."

"Your friends in the Bureau want her to stay." This time he didn't attempt to disguise the bitterness in his voice. "They don't want anything to interfere with the investigation at this delicate state," he quoted, jamming a cigarette between his lips. "As long as she's willing to cooperate, they won't move her."

"And Jessica's willing to cooperate."

"She's a stubborn, thick-headed fool who's too busy thinking about Adams and Ryce and that precious shop of hers."

"You've gotten to know her, I see," the commissioner commented. "Does she trust you?"

Slade expelled a stream of smoke. "She trusts me."

"Keep her in the house, Slade. In her room if you think it's necessary. The servants can think she's ill."

"I want—"

"What you want isn't the issue," Dodson cut him off curtly. "Or what I want," he added more calmly. "If it's gone far enough that a pro was hired, she'll be safer there, with you, than anyplace else. We've got to nail this down fast, with luck, before it's known that the contract on her is no longer operable."

"She's nothing more than bait," Slade said bitterly.

"Just make sure she isn't swallowed," Dodson retorted. "You've got your orders."

"Yeah. I've got them." Disgusted, Slade slammed down the receiver. Looking down at his hands, he realized, frustrated, that they were as good as tied. He was up against a solid wall of refusal from Jessica right on down. The investigation, the justice of it, didn't matter to him any longer. She was all that mattered. That in itself destroyed his objectivity, and by doing so, made her vulnerable. He cared too much to think logically.

His hands curled into fists. No, *cared* wasn't the right word, he admitted slowly. He was in love with her. When or how, he didn't have the faintest idea. Maybe it had started that first day she had come tearing down the steps toward him. And it was stupid.

He scraped his hands roughly over his face. Even without the mess they were in, it was stupid. They'd been born on opposite sides of the fence, had lived their entire lives on opposite sides of the fence. He didn't have any right to love her, even less to want her to love him. She needed him now, professionally as well as emotionally. That would change when it was over.

Right now he couldn't afford to think of how he would deal with his feelings once Jessica was safe again. First he had to make certain she would be. With slow, deliberate force he crushed out his cigarette, then went upstairs to her.

They came into the bedroom together, Jessica from the bath, Slade from the hall. She was wrapped in one of the ivory towels with the pale green border. Her hair fell wet around her shoulders while the clean, sharp scent of soap surrounded her. Her skin was flushed and glowing from the heat of her bath.

For a moment they stood still, watching each other. She could feel the frustration, the anger in him, as he turned to close the door behind him.

"Are you all right?"

"Yes." She sighed a little because it was nearly the truth. "I'm better. Don't be angry with me, Slade."

"Don't ask for the impossible."

"All right." Needing something to do, she went to the dresser and picked up her brush. "What do we do now?"

"We wait." Straining against impotence, he jammed his fists in his pockets. "You're to stay in the house, let the servants think you're ill or tired or just plain lazy. You're not to answer the door, or the phone, or see anyone unless I'm with you."

She slammed the brush back down, her eyes meeting his in the mirror. "I won't be jailed in my own home."

"Either that or a cell," he improvised, adding a shrug. "Either way you want it."

"You can't put me in a cell."

"Don't bet on it." Leaning back against the door, he ordered his muscles to relax. "You're going to play this my way, Jess. Starting now."

Her automatic rebellion was instantly quelled as she remembered those agonizing minutes on the beach. She wasn't only risking her own life, she realized, but his as well. "You're right," she murmured. "I'm sorry." Abruptly she whirled around. "I *hate* this! I hate all of it."

"I told Betsy you didn't want to be disturbed," he answered calmly. "She's got it into her head that you've caught a touch of David's flu. We'll let her go on thinking it. Why don't you get some sleep?"

"Don't go," she said quickly as he reached for the doorknob.

"I'll just be down in the library. You need to rest, Jess, you're worn out."

"I need you," she corrected and walked to him. "Make love to me, Slade . . . as if we were just a man and a woman who wanted to be together." Lifting her arms, she circled his neck. "Can't we believe that it's true for just a few hours? Let's give each other the rest of the morning."

He lifted the back of his hand to her cheek in a gesture they both found uncharacteristic. Slade wondered if she knew that his need was as great as hers—to touch, to lose himself in lovemaking. So close, he thought as he ran his knuckles over the line of her cheekbone. He'd come so close to losing her.

"Your eyes are shadowed." His voice was rough with emotion. "You should rest." But his lips were already lowering to seek hers.

The brush of mouth on mouth—gentle, caring, comforting. Jessica melted against him, overpowered by the tenderness she'd drawn out of him. His hand was still on her face, gliding over her features as if to memorize them. On a sigh, her lips parted, softening under his until he thought he would sink into them.

They had stood there only the night before, locked in an embrace that had been turbulent with passion, almost brutal with desire. The soothing quality of his kiss was no less arousing.

The pulse at the base of her throat beat thickly as Slade's fingertip slid down to it. She needed, he needed. Thinking only of this, he brought his hand to the loose knot of the towel to draw the material from her before he carried her to bed.

Jessica saw his eyes, dark and intense, sweep over her as she began to unbutton his shirt. Then her fingers were trapped between their bodies, his mouth fixed on hers again. The night before, he'd made her soar; now he made her float. Soft kisses, soft words, both unexpected, rained over her. His fingers combed through her damp hair, spreading it out on the pillow, lingering in its silk as if he would touch each individual strand.

Her hands were free again and, trembling, they dealt with the last buttons on his shirt. She felt a quiver race after her exploring hands, heard his incoherent murmur as she worked the rest of his clothes from him. Flesh to heated flesh, they began the journey. Rain began to patter against the windows.

He'd never been a gentle lover—intense, yes, passionate, yes, but never gentle. She unlocked something in him, something giving and tender. No less desperately than the night before, he wanted her, but with the hunger came the sweet calming breath of love. The peaceful emotion guided them both to meet the unspoken needs of the other. *Touch me here. Let me taste. Look at me.* There was no need for words when hearts and minds were attuned.

He wandered over the body he already knew so well. In the gray, gloomy light he worshiped her with hands, lips, and eyes. Naked, heavy eyed, skin flushed with desire, Jessica lay quietly as he took his gaze over her with the slow intensity she recognized. She was a willing prisoner in the thick, humming world conceived by pleasure and sensation. The rain grew loud, the room dimmer.

Lifting a hand to either side of his face, she drew him back to her. With her tongue, she slowly traced the shape of his mouth, then probed inside to drink up all the tastes of him. Flavors musky and sharp seeped into her, deep into her, until she hungered for more. Desire rose to the next plane.

Not so gentle now, nor so calmly, they sought each other. Kisses became possessive, caresses urgent. Under the sound of the rain she heard his breath shudder. Under the pressure of her hands, she felt his muscles tighten. The liquefying pleasure that had ruled her became a hot, torrid need, catapulting her beyond the gray, insular room into a place of white light and golden fire.

Searing, searching, seducing, his mouth veered down her, over her, until her skin was molten. With a strength only recently discovered, she rolled on top of him to complete a crazed journey of her own. They tangled and untangled in a wildly choreographed dance of passion. The light wasn't white now, but red; the fire flamed blue.

She heard her name rip from his lips before they crushed down on hers. Whatever madness he spoke was muffled against her in his urgency. Desire spun into delirium as they came together. There was speed and strength and desperation. Faster and faster they climbed while his mouth clung to hers, swallowing her gasps, mixing them with his own.

Spent, she lay beneath him. His mouth was pressed to her throat, his hands tangled in her hair. The rain drummed against the windows now, hurled by the wind. His body was warm and damp and heavy on hers. A feeling of security drifted over her, followed by a weariness that reached her bones. Slade lifted his head to see her eyes glazed over with fatigue.

"You'll sleep now." It wasn't a question. He tempered the command with a kiss.

"You'll stay?" The words were thick as she fought off sleep long enough to hear his answer.

"I'll start the fire." Rising, Slade walked to the white brick hearth and added paper to the kindling. The long match hissed as he struck it. Crouched, he watched the flames lick, then catch.

Minutes passed, but he remained, staring steadily at the fire without seeing it. He knew what was happening to him. No, what had happened to him, Slade corrected. He was in love with a woman he should never have touched. A woman he had no business loving. A woman, he reminded himself grimly, whose life depended on him. Until she was out of danger, he couldn't afford to think of his own feelings, or of their consequences. For her sake, the cop had to come first, the man second.

Straightening, he turned back to her. The shock of the morning had taken its toll in exhaustion, he noted. She lay on her stomach, one hand balled loosely on the pillow. Her hair fanned out, dry now, her face pale beneath its disorder. Her eyes were shadowed, her breathing heavy. The fire brought flickers of light into the room to play over her skin.

She was too small, he thought, too slender, to deal

with what had happened; to deal with the threat of what could happen. And how much good would he do her? he asked himself as his eyes passed over her. Love clouded his judgment, slowed his reflexes. If he'd been an instant slower that morning. . . . Shaking his head, Slade began to dress. It wouldn't happen again. He'd keep her in the house if he had to chain her. He'd see her through this, keep her safe, and then . . .

Then he'd get out of her life, he promised himself. And get her out of his.

He drew the sheet over her, allowing his hand to linger on her hair briefly before he left the room.

Chapter 7

Late, late in the morning, while Jessica slept, Slade stood at the library window that faced the garden. Watery sunlight struggled through the clouds to fall on the wet shrubs and grass. Rosebushes were naked and thorny. Fall flowers hung heavy-headed and dripping, their petals scattered. The storm had stripped the leaves away from the trees so that they lay soggy and dull on the ground. The wind had died.

Someone had let Ulysses out. The dog lumbered along on the wet ground, sniffing here and there without any apparent interest. Finding a likely branch, he clamped it between his teeth, then trotted off toward the beach. Hell of a watchdog, Slade thought in disgust. But then, who could blame the dog for not barking at someone he knew—someone he'd seen in the house for years?

Scrubbing his face with his hands, Slade turned

away from the window. The waiting was eating at him—another sign that he was losing his objectivity. By rights he should have taken this part of the assignment in his stride. As long as Jessica did what she was told, there was virtually no way for anyone on the outside to get to her. The man who had been in the parlor the night before was running scared and for that reason wouldn't test his luck during the day in a house full of active servants. If everything went according to plan, it was simply a matter of holding tight until the FBI made its move. *If*, Slade thought tightly, everything went according to plan. Plans had a way of veering off course when the human element was involved.

A glance at his watch told him that Jessica had been asleep for half an hour. With luck, she'd sleep through the day. When she slept, she was safe—and every hour that she was safe brought them closer to the finish.

Idly, he picked up one of the books from a pile he'd begun to organize. She'd have to get someone to take care of this mess, he thought—once her life was settled again. Once her life was settled, he repeated silently, and he was back in New York, away from her. With an oath, he tossed the book aside. Was he ever going to get away from her? he wondered with something uncomfortably close to fear. Oh, he could put the distance between them—miles of distance. All he had to do was to get into his car and head it in the right direction. But how long would it take him to chase her out of his head? That was for tomorrow, he reminded himself and was suddenly, abominably tired. He knew better than to think of tomorrows.

"Slade?"

Turning, he saw Jessica in the doorway. It annoyed him that she was there, infuriated him that her face was still pale, her eyes still shadowed. "What are you doing up?" he demanded. "You look like hell."

Jessica managed a weak smile. "Thanks. You know how to boost a woman's morale, Sergeant."

"You're supposed to be resting," he reminded her.

"I couldn't sleep."

"Take a pill."

"I never take pills." Because her hands were clammy, she linked them together. She wouldn't tell him of the nightmare that had woken her—of the sharp, sweating fear that had had her choking back a scream as she fought off sleep. Nor would Jessica tell him how she had reached for him only to find him gone. "Are you working?"

Slade frowned, then followed her gaze to the pile of books beside him. "I might as well clear up some of this," he said with a shrug. "I've got nothing but time now."

"I could help." Uncomfortably aware that her movements were jerky, Jessica walked farther into the room. "And don't make one of those snide remarks," she continued hurriedly. "I know the library's a disgrace and the finger points at me, but I do have a knack for organizing once I get started. If nothing else I can fetch and carry for you until—"

He cut off her stream of hasty words by putting his hand over hers as she reached for a book. Her skin was ice cold. Instinctively he tightened his grip, wanting to warm her. "Jess, go back to bed. Get some sleep. I'll have Betsy bring you up a tray later."

"I'm not sick!" The words erupted from her as she yanked her hand away.

"You're going to be," Slade returned evenly, "if you don't take care of yourself."

"Stop treating me like a child," she ordered, enunciating each word carefully. "I don't need a baby sitter."

"No?" He gave a quick laugh, remembering his early conception of his assignment. "Then tell me, how much sleep have you had in the last two days? When's the last time you've had a meal?"

"I had dinner last night," she began.

"You pushed your dinner around your plate last night," he corrected. "Keep it up. You'll pass out and make my job easier."

"I'm not going to pass out," she said quietly. Her eyes had darkened, that much more of a contrast to her skin.

Because he wanted to rage at her, Slade withdrew. "I wouldn't count on it but suit yourself," he said carelessly. "Overall it doesn't matter whether you're conscious or unconscious." In dismissal, he turned back to the stack of books.

"I'm sorry I'm not as accustomed to this sort of thing as you are," Jessica began in a tone that started off calm, then became more and more agitated. "It isn't every day I'm investigated by the FBI and shot at by a professional gunman. The next time I'm sure I'll be able to enjoy a banquet after I see a dead body on my property. All in a day's work for you, isn't it, Slade? Killing a man?"

A hard knot lodged in his stomach, another in his chest. Casually, he pulled out a cigarette and lit it.

Chest heaving with the emotion of her words, she watched him. "Don't you feel *anything?*" Jessica demanded.

He made himself take a long slow drag, made himself speak calmly. "What do you want me to feel? If I'd been slower, I'd be dead."

Swiftly, she turned away, then pressed her forehead to the window glass. The few clinging raindrops blurred and seemed to multiply until she shut her eyes. *And so would you,* she reminded herself. What he did, he did for you. "I'm sorry," she murmured. "I'm sorry."

"Why?" His voice was as cool as the pane she rested upon. And just as hard. "You were on target again."

Taking a deep breath, Jessica turned to face him. Yes, the guards were there, but she knew him better now. What he had done that morning hadn't been done coldly. "You hate being reminded that you're just as human as the rest of us, don't you? It infuriates you that you're haunted by feelings, emotions, needs." Slowly she walked to him. "I wonder if that's why you won't stay with me after we've made love. Are you afraid I'll find a weakness, Slade? A little crack I might be able to widen?"

"Watch how far you go," he warned softly. "You won't like the trip back."

"You hate wanting me, don't you?"

In a deliberately controlled movement, Slade crushed out his cigarette. "Yes."

As she opened her mouth to speak again, the door to the library swung open. Both she and Slade turned to see David stride in. He took a long look at Jessica, then pushed his glasses back up on his nose.

"You look like hell. Why aren't you in bed?"

"David." She couldn't control the tremor in her voice or the sudden urge that had her racing into his arms to hug him fiercely. David sent Slade a surprised look over her shoulder as he awkwardly patted her back.

"What's all this? You got a fever? Come on, Jessie."

Not him, she thought desperately. Please, God, not David. Through sheer force of will, Jessica controlled the tears that burned in her eyes.

In silence, Slade watched the exchange. Jessica clung to David's thin frame as if it were an anchor while he looked puzzled, concerned, and embarrassed all at once. Speculating, Slade dipped his hands into his pockets.

"Hey, what's all this? Is she delirious?" David tossed the question at Slade, but managed to nudge Jessica back enough to peer into her face. "You look ready to drop," he stated and tested her forehead with his palm. "Mom called me at the shop, giving me all kinds of grief about passing on my germs." Drawing her away, he grimaced at the memory. "That's what you get for coming into my room and shoving that chicken soup down my throat."

"I'm all right," she managed. "Just a little tired."

"Sure, tell that to someone who didn't spend last week flat on his back moaning."

Jessica wanted to cling to him again, to pour out everything that was inside her. Instead she took a step back, smiled, and hated herself. "I'll be fine. I'm just going to take it easy for a couple of days."

"Have you called the doctor?"

"David—"

The annoyance in her tone pleased him. "It's great having the situation reversed," he told Slade. "She did nothing but nag for two weeks. Have you?" he demanded of Jessica again.

"When I need one, I'll call one. Why aren't you at the shop?"

"Don't worry, I'm heading right back." David shot her a grin, relieved by the question and the brisk tone. That was more like Jessica. "After Mom called and read me the riot act, I wanted to check on you. The deliveries went out yesterday without any problem. Traffic's been light, but I've made enough sales to earn my keep." He gave her hair a quick tug. "I don't want to see you in the shop until next week, babe. Michael and I can handle it. In fact, you look like you could use a vacation."

"If you tell me how terrible I look again, you're not going to get that raise you've been hinting about."

"That's what happens when you work for a woman," he told Slade. Turning, David headed back for the door. "Mom says for you two to come in to lunch. This time *you're* getting the chicken soup." With a satisfied grin tossed over his shoulder, he left them.

The moment the door closed, Jessica pressed both hands to her mouth. What ran through her wasn't pain, not even an ache, but a bloodless kind of hurt that left her numb in the vital areas of heart and mind.

She didn't move or make any sound. For a moment she felt that she had simply ceased to exist.

"Not David." Her own whispered words jolted her. With them came a torrent of emotion. *"Not David!"* she repeated, whirling on Slade. "I won't believe it. Nothing you can say will make me believe he'd do anything to hurt me. He isn't capable, any more than Michael is."

"In a couple of days it'll be over." Slade kept his tone neutral. "Then you'll know one way or the other."

"I know *now!*" Spinning around, she dashed for the door. Slade's hand clamped down on hers on the handle.

·"You're not going after him," he said evenly. When she tried to jerk free, he took her by the shoulders with more gentleness than he was feeling. He hated to see her like this, tormented, desperate—hating knowing it was him she would turn against. But he had no choice. "You're not going after him," he said again, spacing the words precisely. "Unless I have your word, I'll cuff you to the bed and lock you in." He narrowed his eyes as her hand struggled beneath his. "I mean it, Jess."

She didn't turn against him, but to him. And that, Slade discovered, was worse. "Not David," she murmured, crumpling into his arms. "Slade, I can't bear it. I think I could stand anything but knowing either one of them was involved with what—with what happened this morning."

She seemed so fragile. He was almost afraid she would shatter if he applied the least pressure. What do I do with her now? he wondered as he laid his cheek on her hair. He knew how to handle her when she was furious. He could even manage her when she dissolved into stormy tears. But what did he do when she was simply limp and totally dependent on him? She was asking him for reassurance he couldn't give, emotion he was terrified to offer.

"Jess, don't do this to yourself. Block it out, a couple of days." He tilted up her chin until their eyes met. He saw trust, and a plea. "Let me take care of you," he heard himself say. "I want to take care of you." He wasn't aware of moving until his lips found hers. Her vulnerability undermined him. To keep her from harm, to shield her from hurt, seemed his only purpose. "Think of me," he murmured, unconsciously speaking the thoughts that raced around in his head. "Only think of me." Slade drew her closer, changing the angle for more soft, nibbling kisses. "Tell me you want me. Let me hear you say it."

"Yes, I want you." Breathless and pliant, she allowed him to give and to take while she remained passive. For the moment Jessica had no strength to offer anything but surrender in return, but it was enough for both of them. In his arms she could almost forget the nightmare, and the reality.

He took her hands and buried his lips in the palm of one, then the other. It surprised her enough to steady rather than arouse her. Slade wasn't a man for endearments, or for typically romantic gestures. Even as the tingle ran up her arms, it occurred to Jessica that her weakness, her despair, only made his difficult job impossible. He'd been wiser than he knew to ask her to think of him. Drawing on her reserves of strength, she straightened her shoulders and smiled at him.

"Betsy has a nasty temper when she has to keep meals waiting."

Gratified, he answered the smile. "Hungry?"

"Yes," she lied.

Jessica managed to eat a little, though the food threatened to stick in her throat. Knowing Slade watched her, she made an effort to appear as though she were enjoying the meal. She talked—rambled—about anything but what was foremost on her mind. Too many topics of conversation could lead back to the shop, to David, to Michael. To the man in the grove. Jessica found herself fighting the inclination to look out the window. To look out only reminded her that she was imprisoned in her own home.

"Tell me about your family," she demanded, almost desperately.

Deciding that it would be better to go along with her pretense than insist she eat or rest, Slade passed her cream for the coffee she was allowing to grow cold. "My mother's a quiet woman—the kind of person who talks only when she has something to say. She likes little things like the figure I bought in your shop and fussy glass. She plays the piano—started taking lessons again last year. The only thing she ever insisted on was that Janice and I learn to play."

"Do you?"

Slade heard the surprise in her voice and gave her a mild scowl. "Badly," he admitted. "She finally gave up on me."

"How does she feel about . . ." Jessica hesitated,

then picked up her spoon to stir her coffee. "About
what you do?"

"She doesn't say." Slade watched her move the
spoon around and around until a tiny whirlpool
formed in the cup. "I wouldn't think it any easier to
be the mother of a cop than the wife of one. But she
manages. She's always managed."

With a nod, Jessica pushed the untouched coffee
aside. "And your sister, Janice . . . you said she was
in college."

"She wants to be a chemist." He gave a quick,
mystified laugh. "She said so after her first day in high
school chemistry. You should see her mixing all those
potions. This tall skinny girl with soft eyes and
beautiful hands—not your average mad scientist. She
blew up our bathroom when she was sixteen."

Jessica laughed—perhaps her first genuine laugh in
twenty-four hours. "Did she really?"

"A minor explosion." Slade passed it off, pleased to
hear the low gurgle that had been so much a part of
her until the day before. "The super wasn't too
impressed with her explanation of unstable com-
pounds."

"One can see his point," Jessica mused. "Where
does she go to school?"

"Princeton. She got a partial scholarship."

And even with that, Jessica reflected, the cost of
tuition must devour his income. How much did a cop
make? she wondered. Not enough, she thought instantly. Not nearly enough to compensate for the risk.
His writing takes a back seat to his sister's education.
Jessica studied the cold coffee in her cup and won-

dered if Janice Sladerman realized how much her brother was willing to sacrifice for her.

"You must love her very much," she murmured. "And your mother."

Slade lifted a brow. It wasn't something he thought of, it simply was. "Yes, I do. Things haven't been easy on either of them. They never complain, never expect."

"And you?" Lifting her eyes, Jessica gave him a long, quiet look. "How have you managed to hide from them what you really want?" Sensing his instant withdrawal, she reached out to take his hand. "You really hate anyone knowing what a nice person you are, don't you, Slade? Doesn't suit the tough cop image." She grinned, pleased to see that she'd embarrassed him. "You can always tell me how you knock suspects around until they beg to confess."

"You've been watching too many old movies." Linking his fingers with hers, Slade drew her to her feet.

"They're one of my vices," she confessed. "I can't tell you how many times I've seen *The Big Sleep*."

"That's about a private detective, not a cop," he pointed out as he walked her back to the library.

"What's the difference?"

He shot her a look. "How much time do you have?"

"Well." She considered, glad to forget the outside world for a few moments. "It might be interesting to learn why one's called a flatfoot and the other a gumshoe."

He stopped, turning to her with an expression

between amusement and exasperation. "Very old movies," he decided.

"Classics," she corrected. "I only watch them for their cultural value."

Slade only lifted a brow at that. It was a gesture Jessica had learned he used in lieu of dozens of words. "Since you want to help, you can do the cataloging." He gestured toward the pile of books littering the work table. "Your handwriting has to be better than mine."

"All right." Grateful for any task, Jessica plucked one of a neat stack of index files. "I suppose you'll want to reference and cross-reference and all that sort of thing."

"Something like that."

"Slade." She put the card back down before she turned to him. "You'd rather be working on your book than doing this. Why don't you take a couple of hours for yourself?"

He thought of the novel, nearly finished, waiting for him on the desk upstairs. Then he thought of the way Jessica had looked when she had walked through the library doors an hour before.

"This kind of mess drives me crazy," he told her. "While I'm here, I might as well point you in the right direction. How many books are in here?" he asked before she could voice another objection.

Momentarily distracted, Jessica looked around. "I don't have any idea. Most of these were my father's. He loved to read." A smile touched her lips, then her eyes. "His taste was eclectic to say the least but I think he had a preference for hard-boiled whodunits." The thought occurred to her quite suddenly. "What's your book about? Is it a detective novel?"

"The one I'm working on now?" He grinned. "No."

"Well?" She lowered a hip to the table. "What then?"

He began to make a clear space for her to work. "It's about a family, beginning in the postwar forties and working through modern day. Changes, adjustments, disappointments, victories."

"Let me read it," she demanded impulsively. His words, she knew instinctively, would reveal much of the inner man.

"It's not finished."

"I'll read what is."

Searching for a pencil, Slade stalled. He wanted his words read. It was a dream he'd lived with for too many years to count. But Jessica was different; she wasn't the nameless, faceless public. Her opinion, good or bad, held too much weight. "Maybe," he muttered. "If you're going to help, you'd better sit down."

"Slade." Wrapping her arms around his waist, Jessica rested her cheek on his back. "I'll just bother you until you say yes. It's a talent of mine."

Something about the casually intimate embrace stirred him beyond belief. Her breasts pressed lightly against his back; her hands linked loosely at his waist. In that moment, for that moment, he surrendered completely to the love he felt for her. It was deeper than need, sharper than longing.

Didn't she see that there was nothing he could

refuse her? Slade thought as he brought his hands down to cover hers. Couldn't she see that she'd become woman and dream and vulnerability, all in the space of days? If they were to pretend—for her sake—that there was no threat beyond the walls, perhaps they could pretend for his that she belonged to him.

"Bother me," he invited, turning so that he could gather her into his arms. "But I warn you, I'm no pushover."

With a low laugh, Jessica rose on her toes until her lips brushed his. "I can only hope my work's cut out for me." Deepening the kiss, she slid her hands under his shirt to run them up the firm planes of his back, along the ridge of muscle.

"That might get you a couple of pages," he murmured. "Want to try for a chapter?"

She allowed her tongue to trace his lips lazily, giving them a quick teasing nip as she slid a finger up and down his spine. She sensed his response, just as she sensed his reluctance to show it to her. "Bargaining is my forte," she told him quietly. She gave him a slow, lingering kiss, retreating just as she felt him increase the pressure. "Just how many chapters are in this book?"

Slade closed his eyes, the better to enjoy the sensation of being seduced when no seduction was necessary. "About twenty-five."

"Hmmm." He felt her lips curve as they touched his again. "This could take all day."

"Count on it." Unexpectedly, he drew her away, then framed her face with his hands. "We can start negotiations right after we do some work in here."

"Oh." Catching her tongue between her teeth, Jessica looked around at the disordered books. "After?"

"After," Slade said firmly, nudging her down in a chair. "Start writing."

Jessica was hardly aware of the hours that passed— one, then two, then three. He worked quietly, systematically, and with a patience she could never hope to emulate. Slade knew the books a great deal better than she. Jessica saved reading for the rare times when her physical energy lagged behind her mental energy. She enjoyed books. He loved them. She found this small realization another step in the ladder to discovering him.

It was easier in the quiet, cluttered library to get him to talk. *Have you read this? Yes. What did you think of it?* And he would tell her, easily and in depth, without ever stopping his work. How her father would have liked him, Jessica thought. He would have admired Slade's mind, his strength, his sudden flashes of humor. He would have seen the goodness Slade took such care to keep hidden.

She doubted Slade realized that, by letting her work with him here, he was revealing his other side. The dreamer. Perhaps she'd always known it was there, even when she had recognized the streak of hard street sense. It was a complex man who could carry a gun and discuss Byron's *Don Juan* with equal ease. That afternoon she needed the dreamer. Perhaps he knew it.

The light began to fade to a soft gray. Shadows gathered in the corners of the room. Jessica had forgotten her tension and had become involved with the mindless task of copying titles and names onto the index cards. When the phone rang, she scattered two dozen of them on the floor. Quickly she began to retrieve them.

"It just startled me," she said when Slade remained silent. She cursed her trembling hands as she gathered the cards back into a pile. "It's been so quiet, that's all." Furious with herself, she let the cards fall again. "Damn it, don't sit there looking at me like that! I'd rather you swore at me."

He rose and went to her, then crouched in front of her. "You made a hell of a mess," he murmured. "If you can't do better, I'll have to get myself a new assistant."

With a sound that was part sigh, part laugh, she leaned her forehead against his. "Give me a break, it's my first day on the job."

Betsy opened the door, then lifted her brows and pursed her lips. Well, she always figured where there was smoke there was fire, and she'd smelled smoke the minute those two had set eyes on each other. She gave a quick harrumph and watched Jessica jump as though she'd been scalded.

"Mr. Adams is on the phone," Betsy said regally, then closed the door again.

Slade closed his hand over Jessica's. "Call her back," he said quietly. "Have her tell him you're resting."

"No." With a quick shake of the head, she rose. "Don't keep asking me to run, Slade, because I might do it. Then I'd hate myself." Turning, she picked up the phone. "Hello, Michael."

Slowly Slade straightened, tucked his hands in his pockets, and watched her.

"No, it's nothing really, just a little touch of the flu." Jessica spoke in quiet tones while she wrapped the phone cord around and around her fingers. "David's just feeling guilty because he thinks I caught it from him. He shouldn't have worried you. I am taking care of myself." She shut her eyes tightly a moment, but her voice remained light and steady. "No, I won't be in tomorrow." The cord of the phone dug into her skin. Carefully Jessica unwound it. "That's not necessary, Michael. . . . No, really. I promise—don't worry. I'll be—I'll be fine in a couple of days. Yes, I will. . . . Good-bye."

After replacing the receiver, Jessica stood for a moment, staring down at her empty hands. "He was concerned," she murmured. "I'm never ill. He wanted to come over and see me, but I put him off."

"Good." Sympathy wouldn't help her now, Slade decided. "We've done enough in here for today. Why don't we go upstairs?" He walked to the door, as if taking her agreement for granted. He opened it, then paused and looked back. She still hadn't moved. "Come on, Jess."

She crossed to him, but stopped at the door. "Michael would do nothing to hurt me," she said without looking at him. "I just want you to understand that."

"As long as you understand that I have to look at everyone as a potential threat," he returned evenly. "You're not to see either one of them—or anyone else—unless I'm with you." Spotting the light of defiance in her eyes, he continued. "If he and David are innocent, the next couple of days won't do them any harm. If you really believe it," he went on, shrugging off the look of fury she sent him, "you should be able to handle all this."

He wasn't going to give her an inch, Jessica concluded as she fought both tears and rage. Perhaps it was best if he didn't. She took a long steadying breath. "You're right. And I will handle it. Are you going to work on your book now?"

Slade gave no sign that the change of subject made any difference to him. "I thought I might."

Jessica was determined to be just as practical as he—at least on the surface. "Fine. Go on up then and I'll bring some coffee for both of us. You can trust me," she went on before he could object. "I'll do exactly what you tell me to do so I can prove you wrong. I *am* going to prove you wrong, Slade," she told him with quiet, concrete determination.

"Fine, as long as you stick to the rules."

Finding herself more at ease with a goal in mind, Jessica smiled. "Then I'll bring up the coffee. While I'm reading your book, you can concentrate on finishing it. It's one sure way to keep me occupied for the rest of the day."

He pinched the lobe of her ear. "Is that a bribe?"

"If you don't know one when you hear one," she countered, "you must be a pretty lousy cop."

Chapter 8

JESSICA'S COFFEE GREW COLD AGAIN. SHE SAT UP against the headboard of Slade's bed with a pile of manuscript on either side of her. The stack of pages she had read was rapidly outgrowing the pile she had yet to read. Engrossed, she had been able to pass off Betsy's nagging when the housekeeper had brought up a tray of soup and sandwiches. Jessica had given her an absent promise to eat which she had forgotten the moment the door was closed again. She'd forgotten, too, though he had scrawled notes and revisions in the margins, that she was reading Slade's work. The story, the people, had completely taken her over.

She traveled with an ordinary family through the postwar forties, through the simplicities and complexities of the fifties, into the sixties with their turbulence and fluctuating mores. Children grew up, values changed. There were deaths and births, the realization of some dreams and the destruction of others. Through it all, as a new generation coped with the pressures of the seventies, Jessica came to know them. They were people she might have met—undeniably people she would have cared for.

The words flowed, at times gently, at other times with a grittiness that made her stomach tighten. It wasn't an easy story—his characters were too genuine for that. He showed her things she didn't always want to be shown, but she never considered setting the pages aside.

At the end of a chapter Jessica reached automatically for the next page. Confused, she glanced down to see that there were no more. Annoyed with the interruption, she then realized she had read all he had given her. For the first time in almost three hours, the sound of Slade's typing penetrated her concentration.

There was a full moon. That, too, came to her abruptly. The light flowed into the room to vie with the stream of the bedside lamp. The fire Slade had lit when they'd come upstairs had burned down to glowing embers. Jessica stretched her cramped muscles, wanting to give herself a moment before she went into Slade.

When she had insisted on reading his work, Jessica hadn't been certain how she would feel or what she would say to him when she was finished. Knowing herself too easily influenced by emotion, she had been certain that she would find some merit in his writing. Now she wanted time to decide how much her feelings for Slade had to do with her feelings about the story she had just read.

None, she realized. Before she had completed the

first chapter Jessica had forgotten why she was reading it even though her main purpose had been accomplished. She knew Slade better now.

He had a depth of perception she had only sensed, an insight into people she envied as well as admired. In his writing as well as his speech, he was frugal with words—but in the writing, his inner thoughts surfaced. He might be sparing with his own emotions, but his characters had a range to them that were rooted in their creator.

And, Jessica mused, she'd been wrong when she had once told him he didn't know women. He knew them—almost too well, she thought as she fingered the tip of a page. How much did he see, when he looked at her, that she had been confident was private? How much did he understand, when he touched her, that she had been certain she could keep hidden?

Did he know she loved him? Instinctively Jessica glanced at the doorway that separated the bedroom and the sitting room. Slade's typing continued. No, she was certain he had no idea how deep her feelings ran. Or, she thought with a small smile, that she was determined not to let him walk out of her life whenever, or however, things were resolved. If he knew, she mused, he'd put her at arm's length. A cautious man, she reflected. Slade was a very cautious man—one who saw himself suited for the solitary life. Jessica decided that he had some surprises coming. When she felt her life was her own again, she was going to deal him a few.

She rose and went to the doorway. His back was to her, the light falling on his hands as they moved over the keys. From the set of his shoulders, the angle of his head, she could tell his concentration was deep. Not wanting to disturb him, she waited, resting against the doorjamb. The ashtray at his elbow was half full, with a lit cigarette smoldering and forgotten. His coffee cup was empty, but his dinner tray hadn't been touched. She felt a Betsy-like urge to scold him for neglecting to eat.

This is how it could be, she realized abruptly, if the nightmare was behind us. He could work here, and I'd hear the sound of his typing when I came home. There'd be times he'd get up in the middle of the night and close the door so the noise wouldn't wake me. We'd walk on the beach on Sunday mornings . . . watch the fire on rainy afternoons. One day, she thought and closed her eyes. It could happen one day.

With an exasperated sigh, Slade stopped typing. One hand reached up to rub at the stiffness in his neck. Whatever impetus had driven him for three hours had suddenly dried up, and he wasn't ready. Automatically he reached for his coffee, only to find the cup empty. Maybe if he went down for some more, the flow would come back. Even as he considered it, Jessica came to him.

Wrapping her arms around his neck, she rested her cheek on top of his head. Love was coursing through her swiftly, too swiftly. She squeezed him tightly, forcing back the words she was afraid he wasn't ready to hear. There were others she wanted to say first.

"Slade, don't ever stop doing what you were meant to do."

Not sure of her meaning, he frowned down at the words he'd just written. "How much did you read?"

"All you gave me—not enough. When will you finish? Oh, Slade, it's wonderful!" Jessica continued before he could speak. "It's a beautiful piece of work. Everything: the words, the feeling, the people."

Slade turned so that he could see her face. He didn't want platitudes, not from her. Her eyes were lit with enthusiasm while his remained cool and guarded. "Why?"

"Because you told a story with depth, about people all of us have met or have been." She spread her fingers, searching for words that would satisfy him. "Because it made me cry, and cringe, and laugh. There were parts—that scene in the parking lot in the seventh chapter—I didn't want to read. It was hard, savage. But I had to read it even when it hurt. Slade, no one that reads that is going to be untouched." She laid her hands back on his shoulders. "And isn't that why a writer writes?"

His eyes never left hers. He waited, weighing what he saw there with her words. "You know," he said slowly, "I don't think I realized until just now what a chance I was taking by letting you read it."

"A chance," she repeated. "Why?"

"If you hadn't been touched, I'm not sure I could have finished it."

Nothing he could have said would have meant more. Jessica brought his hand up to her cheek, wondering if he realized how much he'd said in one sentence. "I was touched, Slade," she said quietly. "When it's published, and I read it, I'm going to remember that part of it was written right here."

"Going to erect a monument?" he asked with a smile.

"Just a discreet plaque." Leaning over, she kissed him. "I wouldn't want it to go to your head. What about an agent?" she asked suddenly. "Do you have one?"

Chuckling, he drew her down into his lap. "Yes, I have one. So far we haven't done each other much good, but he's marketed some short stories, and he's doing whatever it is agents do to sell my other novel."

"The other one." Jessica drew away as Slade began to nibble on her ear. "It's finished then?"

"Mmm-hmm. Come back here," he demanded, wanting to taste that soft, sensitive spot at the curve of her shoulder.

"What's it about?" she demanded, eluding him. "When can I read it? Is it as good as this one?"

"Has anyone ever told you that you ask too many questions?" His hand slipped under her sweater to cup her breast. With his thumb, he flicked lazily over the point, feeling it harden as her heartbeat went from steady to erratic. "I like that," he murmured, nipping at the cord of her neck. "I can feel your pulse go crazy everywhere I touch." In one long stroke, he moved down her rib cage to her waist. "You're losing weight," he said with a frown. "You're already too thin. Did you eat any dinner?"

"Has anyone ever told you that you talk too much?" Jessica asked before she pressed her lips to his.

His answer was a low sound of pleasure. She tasted warm—more pungent than sweet—as the tip of her tongue slipped to his to tantalize, then retreated to provoke. He thought he heard her laugh, low and husky, before he gripped the back of her neck in his hand and plunged deep. Her scent and her taste were the same so that he felt himself surrounded by her. Before Slade could rise to carry her to the bed, Jessica was pulling him to the floor.

There was a sudden urgency in her, a flash of fire. The habitual energy that had been lacking in her all day abruptly surfaced in a torrent of passion. She tugged at the buttons of his shirt, impatient to have his flesh against hers while her mouth was already making wild passes over his face and throat. Her aggression both unbalanced and aroused him. Because he understood that part of it came from a need to block out her fears, Slade let her lead. The pace was hers—and it was frantic.

Within moments he was too caught up in her to think at all. She was undressing him swiftly, her lips following the path of her busy hands until his mind was totally centered on her. Shivering thoughts, quick tastes, maddening touches—she gave him no time to focus on only one, but insisted he experience all in an enervating haze of sensation.

Vulnerability was something new to him, but he found himself trapped in a sultry, viscous world where he had no guards, no defense. She was driving him beyond the point of reason, but still he couldn't find the will to stop her and take command. This time there was only response. It poured from him, increasing her strength and depleting his.

When her mouth fixed on his again, he fumbled with her sweater. He, whose hands were always sure, found them damp and trembling when at last he could touch her. Though her flesh was as hot as his, she allowed him to linger nowhere, moving over him with a speed and agility that left his hands frustrated and his body throbbing. Skin slid over skin, her moïst, hungry mouth ravaging, her soft hands greedy.

Knowing he was helpless excited her. This strong man, this hard man, was completely powerless under her spell. But Jessica had no spells, only needs. And love. She realized that she loved him more on finding that he could be weak. His body was firm and muscled, but it shuddered now—for her.

The light from the desk lamp slanted across his face so that she could see his eyes, opaque with passion, on hers. His mouth was tempting, and she took it, tasting all the hot, heady flavors that sprang from desire. His breath was warm and ragged as it trembled into her open mouth. With sudden clarity, she smelled the lemon and beeswax polish from the desk. In some sane portion of her mind, Jessica knew the scent would come back to her whenever she thought of the first time he fully gave himself to her. For she had him now—mind, emotion, and body. Even when he took them back, she would have had this one instant in time when he held nothing away from her.

So she gave herself to him, taking him into her on a flash of sharp silvery pleasure. Her strength soared, driving both of them fast and hard, until it crested, suspending them. When it ebbed, she seemed to dissolve into him so that they lay entwined, joined and sated.

Slade struggled to clear his mind but found that she filled it, consumed it. The power that had driven her was depleted, her body nearly weightless on his, but he discovered that she still dominated him. He wanted to draw away, perhaps to prove to both of them that he could, that he had a choice. His hands only tangled deeper into her hair until he found the soft, slender neck. Though she lay passive, hardly breathing, he could feel the hammer of her heart against his. No force of will could make his pulses level though his physical need was fully satisfied. He wanted her—but his wants were only to have her near.

"Jess." He lifted her face to his without any idea what thoughts would spill out into words. Her eyes were huge and heavy and shadowed. Her face was soft, with the afterglow of passion and with weariness. He'd had no right, he thought on a quick rage of guilt, no right to allow her to use up all her reserves of energy and strength to satisfy his needs.

"No, don't." Jessica could see the change in his face. Already, she thought, he was taking back what he had so briefly given her. "Don't shut me out," she said quietly. "Don't shut me out so soon."

Without realizing he was doing so, he traced her lips with his thumb. "Sleep with me tonight" was all he said.

Slade waited until he was certain she slept before he eased from the bed. Watching Jessica, he dressed in silence. Thin moonlight washed over her face and bare shoulders, shifting with shadows as a cloud passed over the moon. With any luck, he calculated that he could give the first floor a thorough check, stake out the parlor for a couple of hours, then be back without her ever knowing he had gone. Giving her one last look, he slipped from the room.

With the soundless efficiency that came from years of experience, Slade tested the multitude of doors and windows. He noted with disgust the simple locks that would keep out only the rankest of amateurs.

The house is full of silver and small, portable valuables, he reflected. A burglar's paradise—and she seals it off with dime-store locks. A credit card and a hairpin, Slade decided as he examined the rear kitchen door. He'd have to see that Jessica installed something less flimsy before he left.

In a mound of white fur, Ulysses slept on the cool tile floor, snoring lightly. He never stirred as Slade stepped over him. Testing, Slade rattled the knob on the back door. Ulysses' rhythm never altered.

"Wake up, you good-for-nothing mutt."

At the command, the dog opened one glazed eye, thumped his tail twice, then went back to sleep.

Rubbing the back of his neck, Slade reminded himself that a run-of-the-mill burglar wasn't the immediate problem. He stepped over the dog again and left him snoring.

Cautiously, he moved through the servants' wing. There was a pale light under one door and the muffled laughter of a late-night talk show. The rest were silent. Glancing at his watch, he saw that it was just past midnight. Slade went back to the parlor to wait.

He sat in a wingback chair, lost in the shadows. Watch and wait. There was little more he could do. And he was itching to do something—anything to move the investigation along. Maybe the commissioner picked the wrong man after all, he mused. This time Slade wanted to look for trouble—and he wanted to find it. Whoever had hired the man in the grove was going to pay, he had little doubt of that. But he wanted to collect personally.

The woman upstairs in his bed was all that mattered. The diamonds were incidental—they were just rocks, after all, with a market value. Jessica was priceless. With a silent laugh, he stretched out his legs. Dodson could hardly have foreseen that his hand-picked bodyguard would fall in love with his assignment. Slade knew his own reputation: thorough, precise, and cool.

Well, he thought, he'd lost his cool almost from the instant he'd seen the little blond whirlwind with the Viking cheekbones. He wasn't thinking like a cop but like a man—a man who wanted revenge. And that was dangerous. As long as he remained on the force, he had to play by the rules. The first rule was no personal involvement.

Slade nearly laughed aloud at that. Rule one down the tubes, he decided as he dragged a hand through his hair. How could he be more personally involved? He was already in love with her, already her lover. If they were any more personal they'd be married and having children.

That thought stopped him cold. He couldn't permit his mind to run in that direction. He wasn't for her. They'd drift apart once the investigation was over. Naturally that's what he wanted, Slade told himself, but the frown remained in his eyes. He had his own life to deal with—the demands of his profession, his responsibilities, his writing. Even if there was room in his life for a woman, their paths ran in opposite directions. They weren't about to cross again. It was only chance that had brought them together this time, circumstances that had brought about an intimacy that had led to emotional attachment. He'd get over her. He pinched the bridge of his nose between his thumb and forefinger. The hell he would.

Wasn't a man allowed a few dreams? he demanded of himself, when he sat alone in the dark in a room that smelled of lemon wax and fall flowers. Wasn't he allowed to weave some sort of future when a woman lay soft and warm in his bed? He was entitled to some basic selfishness, wasn't he? With a half sigh, Slade settled against the back of the chair. Maybe the man was, but the cop wasn't. And, he reminded himself, Jessica needed the cop more whether she believed it or not.

Blanking out his mind, Slade waited in the dark for just under three hours. Instinct told him he was wasting his time. Some sleep was essential if he was to be alert enough to keep her safe and occupied during the daylight hours. Stiff from sitting, he absently worked out the kinks as he headed back to the stairs. Another day, he mused, two at the most—if Agent Brewster was as close as he'd led Slade to believe.

Fatigue settled over him the moment he allowed his muscles to relax. Four hours' sleep would recharge his system—he'd gotten by on less. Quietly, he turned the knob of his bedroom door.

Jessica was sitting in the middle of the bed, curled into a tight ball. She took the deep, tearing breaths of a drowning woman fighting for air. Moonlight pooled over her as she shuddered.

"Jess?"

There was a scream rising in her throat. When her

head jerked up, Slade saw the wild sheen of fear in her eyes before she focused on him. She could hold back the cry by digging her teeth into her lip, but the shudders went on. Slade went to her swiftly. Her skin was clammy as he took her shoulders; her face damp with a mixture of tears and perspiration. It ran through his mind that someone had slipped past him and gotten to her, then the idea was as quickly dismissed.

"What is it?" he demanded. "What's the matter?"

"It's nothing." Desperately she fought to control the tremors. The nightmare had come back, horridly vivid, to attack all of her senses. Cold wind, the smell of salt spray, the roar of the surf—and someone's heavy footsteps as they ran after her, the shifting shadows as clouds blocked out the sun, the iron taste of her own terror. And worse, much worse, she had been afraid to turn, afraid she would see the face of someone loved on the man who pursued her.

"I woke up," she managed. "I guess I panicked when you weren't here." It was partially true and difficult enough to confess. She couldn't bring herself to admit she could be terrorized by a dream.

"I was just downstairs." He brushed sweat-dampened hair from her cheeks. "I wanted to make sure everything was locked up."

"Professional habit?" She nearly managed a smile before she dropped her head to his shoulder.

"Yeah." Even as he gathered her close, she trembled. It wasn't the moment, he decided, to lecture her on flimsy locks and thin chains. "I'll go down and get you a brandy."

"No!" She bit her lip again as the refusal came out too forcefully. "No, please, I already feel like an idiot."

"You're entitled to be jumpy, Jess." Softly, he brushed a kiss over her hair.

She wanted to cling, to beg him not to leave her alone for an instant. She wanted to pour out every fear and fantasy and dread. But she couldn't, and the denial was as much for her own sake as his. "With a policeman in the house?" she countered. Tilting back her head, she looked up at him. A strong face, she mused. Strong arms and serious eyes. "Just come to bed; you must be tired." Making the effort, she forced away the nerves and gave him a smile. "How does one man cope with two careers, Sergeant?"

He shrugged as he kneaded her tense shoulders. "I manage. How can a woman look so beautiful at three o'clock in the morning?"

"My mother claims it's bone structure." Her smile warmed a bit as she willed herself to relax under his hands. "I prefer to think it's something less scientific . . . like being born during a lunar eclipse."

Nuzzling her neck, he chuckled. "Were you?"

"Yes. My father said that's why I had cat's eyes—to help me see in the dark."

Slade kissed her lightly before he set her away from him and rose. "If you don't get some sleep, they're going to be bloodshot."

"What a gallant thing to say." Jessica frowned at him as he undressed. "What about you?"

"I can get by on three or four hours when I have to."

She gave a quick snort. "Your machismo's surfacing, Slade."

When he turned his head, the moonlight streamed over his face, illuminating the lightning-fast grin. Jessica felt her heart flutter up to her throat. Shouldn't she be used to him by now? she wondered. The mercurial moods, the streaks of boyish good humor in the sometimes overly serious man? His body was sleek and limber, streamlined like a Channel swimmer's, muscled like a lightweight boxer's. His face mirrored both of his professions—the intellect and the action.

He'll take care of you, her mind comforted. Just trust. But there were lines of fatigue and strain that the moonlight accented as well. *And you take care of him,* her thoughts added. Smiling, she held out her arms to him.

"Come to bed," she ordered.

Lying down beside her, Slade drew her close. There was no driving physical need to possess her. Instead he felt a simple serenity, all the more precious for its rarity. For the next few hours they would be any man and woman sharing the intimacy of sleep. She curled warmly into him, as much to soothe as be soothed. There were no more words.

Jessica lay still, schooling her breathing so that it was deep and even until she felt him drift off. With her eyes open and fear threatening on the verges of her mind, she watched the moonlight play on his shoulder as it rose and fell. The light was misty with predawn before she slept.

* * *

When the phone rang, he jolted out of a restless sleep. Sweat pearled on his forehead. Afraid to answer, more afraid not to, he lifted the receiver. "Yes, hello."

"Your time's up."

"I need more," he said quickly. Knowing that weakness would never be tolerated, he swallowed the tremor in his voice. "Just a few days. . . . It isn't easy to get to them with the house full of people."

"Must I remind you that you aren't paid to do only what's easy?"

"I tried to get to them last night . . . I was nearly caught."

"Then you were careless. I've no use for carelessness."

Less for carelessness than weakness, he thought rapidly and moistened his lips. "Jessica—Jessica's not feeling well." He reached for a cigarette to steady his nerves. He had to think quickly and calmly if he wanted to stay alive. "She isn't planning on coming into the shop. In a couple of days I should be able to convince her to take a long weekend. She'll listen to me." He took a greedy drag of his cigarette, praying that he spoke the truth. "With her out of the house, I can get to the diamonds without taking any chances." Moisture beaded on his top lip and he wiped the back of his hand across it. "You'll have them this weekend. A couple of days won't matter."

A sigh breathed through the phone, chilling him. "You're mistaken again—too many mistakes, my young friend. Remember my associate in Paris? He made mistakes."

The phone slid wetly in his hand. He remembered

the man found floating in the Seine. "Tonight," he said desperately. "I'll have them for you tonight."

"Ten o'clock at the shop." He paused to make certain the weapon of fear had done its work. The soft, jerky breathing pleased him. "If you fail this time, I won't be so . . . understanding. You've done very well since you started to work for me. I'd hate to lose you."

"I'll bring them. Then I—then I want out."

"We'll discuss it. Ten o'clock." With a gentle click, the connection was broken.

Chapter 9

Slade's mind and body awoke at the same instant. The luxury of drifting slowly awake was something he had forfeited years before. He had had to perfect the ability to sleep quickly and lightly and to awake just as quickly, ready to function. It was a habit he looked forward to breaking without really believing he ever would.

He saw from the slant of the sun that it was still early, but shifted his gaze to check the mantel clock nonetheless. Just past seven. The four hours' rest had done all it needed to do.

Turning his head, he looked down at Jessica. The pale blue smudges under her eyes made him frown. Though by his calculations she had slept nearly eight hours, the smudges were deeper than they had been the day before. Today he'd make certain she rested more—if he had to slip a sleeping pill into her coffee.

And ate something—if he had to force-feed her. He could all but feel the pounds slipping off her.

Though he barely shifted the mattress as he moved away from her, her hand tightened on his arm. Her eyes flew open. "Get some more sleep," he ordered, touching his lips to hers.

"What time is it?" Her voice was husky and thick, but her hand stayed firm on his arm.

"Early."

Jessica relaxed, muscle by muscle, but didn't release him. "How early?"

"Too early." He bent to give her another brief kiss before he rose, but she pulled him closer.

"Too early for what?"

She felt his lips curve against hers. "You're not even awake yet."

"Wanna bet?" Running a hand down, she trailed her fingers over his flat stomach. The sleepy kiss smoldered with burgeoning passion. "Maybe you can't get by on three or four hours' sleep after all."

Cocking his brow, he lifted his head. "Wanna bet?"

Her answering laugh was smothered by his lips.

It had never been like this for her. Each time they made love it stunned her, enticed her, then consumed her. In his arms, with his hands and lips running wild and free over her body, she could lose herself. And how she needed to lose herself.

He'd known from the first how to play her. Each time they came together he found new variations, giving her no opportunity to become familiar with a touch or to anticipate a demand. He could dominate her mind so effortlessly, plunge her back into a world that was all keen emotion and sharp sensation.

Everything would magnetize, from the bare brush of a fingertip to the bruising pressure of lips. Jessica thought she could feel the individual threads of the sheet against the naked flesh of her back. The whispering tick of the clock was like thunder. Pale sunlight danced, gray and ghostly. She could see it fall over his hair, accenting its dark confusion as she dove her hands into it.

In her ear he whispered something poetic and foolish about the texture of her skin. Though the tone was almost reverent, his hands were aggressive—arousing and drugging in turns. Murmuring, she told him what she wanted. Shifting, she offered what he needed.

When he took her, Slade took her slowly, watching the flickers of pleasure and passion on her face in the thin morning light. Savoring the sensations that rippled through him as she moved, he nibbled on her parted lips. He tasted her, and himself, before he roamed over her closed lids. Fragile, he thought, her skin was so fragile. Yet all the while her hips urged him to take, to take quickly. With iron control he kept the rhythm easy, prolonging the ultimate delight.

"Jess." He could hardly form her name between labored breaths. "Open your eyes, Jess. I want to see your eyes." The lids fluttered, as if weighed down by the pale gold lashes. "Open your eyes, love, and look at me."

He wasn't a man for endearments. Even through the haze of needs and sensations, Jessica recognized it. A new warmth filled her—pure emotion—to double the physical ecstasy. She opened them.

The irises were opaque, rich amber filmed over with passion. As he moved inside her, the lashes flickered, threatening to lower again. "No, look at me." His voice had dropped to a rough whisper. Their lips were close so that their breath merged, shudder for shudder. Jessica saw that his eyes were dark, dark gray and intense, as if he would look into her mind and read whatever frantic thoughts raced inside. "Tell me that you need me," he demanded. "I have to hear you say it, just once."

Jessica struggled to form words as she climbed higher toward delirium. "I need you, Slade . . . you're the only one."

His lips crushed down on hers to muffle her cry as he drove her swiftly to the peak. His last rational thought was almost a prayer—that the words he had demanded would be enough for him.

Strange that his body felt more rested, more relaxed now than it had upon waking. Slade slid down to press a kiss at the hollow between her breasts before he shifted from her. "Now, get some more sleep," he ordered, but before he could rise, Jessica had her arms locked around his neck.

"I've never been more awake in my life. What're you going to do with me today, Slade? Make me fill out more of those silly cards?"

"Those silly cards," he said as he slipped a hand under her knees, "are a necessary part of any organized library."

"They're boring," she said defiantly when he lifted her.

"Spoiled," he decided, carrying her into the bathroom.

"I certainly am not." The line appeared between her brows as he switched on the shower.

"You certainly are," he corrected genially. "But that's all right, I kind of like you that way."

"Oh well, thanks a lot."

He grinned, kissed her, then set her down in the shower stall. Jessica let out one long surprised scream. "*Slade!* It's freezing!"

"Best way to get the blood moving in the morning." He stepped in with her, partially blocking the spray. "Well, second best," he amended, then cut off a stream of abuse with his lips.

"Turn on the hot water," she demanded when he let her breathe again. "I'm turning blue."

He picked up her arm, giving it a light pinch. "No, not yet," he disagreed. "Want the soap?"

"I'll go take my own shower, thanks." Huffily, she tried to climb out only to find herself tangled with him under the icy spray. "Let go! This is police brutality." She lifted her face to glare at him and got struck fully with the cold needle spray. "Slade!" Sputtering, she blinked her eyes to clear them. Her body was pressed against his, frigid and tingling. "You're going to pay for this, I swear you are."

Blinded by the water and her own streaming hair, she struggled to free herself. With one arm keeping her prisoner, Slade took his free hand over her, lavishly soaping her skin.

"Stop it!" Infuriated and aroused, Jessica fought against him. When his hand passed intimately over her bottom, she grew more desperate. Then she heard him chuckle. Temper had her head snapping back up though the spray made her vision vague and watery.

"You listen to me," she began. Soapy fingers passed over her nipple. "Slade, don't." With a moan, she arched away. His palm slipped between her thighs. "No."

But her mouth blindly sought his. Jessica no longer felt the cold.

When she left the shower, she was glowing. Some color had seeped back into her cheeks. Slade noted it with a mixture of relief and pleasure though Jessica did her best to maintain outward indignance.

"I'm going to go get dressed," she informed him as she wrapped her wet hair in a towel. Because she was still naked, Slade found it hard to be offended by her haughty tone. Refreshed, he hooked his own towel around his waist.

"Okay, I'll meet you downstairs for breakfast in ten minutes."

"I'll be there," she told him grandly as she stooped to pick up his shirt, "when I get there."

Grinning, he watched her slip into his shirt and button it. "I could get used to seeing you like that," he commented. When she sent him an arch look, his grin only widened. "Wet and half naked," he explained.

"It's that machismo again," Jessica muttered, holding back the smile. Turning, she flounced to the door.

"Ten minutes," he reminded her.

Jessica cast a baleful look over her shoulder, then slammed the door behind her. Her grin quickly escaped, then almost as quickly faded. David stood directly outside her own bedroom door, his hand already poised to knock. His head had turned at the sound of the slam, but he hadn't moved. His eyes roamed over her, taking in Slade's shirt, the damp, glowing skin and sleep-starved eyes.

"Well." His tone, like his eyes, turned cool. "I guess you're already up."

Jessica felt more color flow into her cheeks. As close as she and David had been, living in the same house, they had never chanced upon each other under these circumstances. Both had always been extremely private about that area of their lives.

We're both adults, Jessica reminded herself as she walked toward him—but they'd been children together.

"Yes, I'm up. Did you want me?" Part of her wanted to run to him as she had the day before; part of her no longer trusted so unconditionally. Guilt gave her a reserve toward him nothing else could have. Sensing it, he became only more distant and disapproving.

"Thought I'd check with you before I went in, that's all." He gave her another brief, telling look. "Since you're busy . . ."

"I'm not busy, David. Come in." Coolly polite, Jessica opened the bedroom door, then gestured him inside. It never occurred to her that she was breaking one of Slade's rules by talking to David alone. Even if it had, she would have done no differently. "Were there any problems yesterday I should know about?"

"No . . ." His eyes rested on the bed, which hadn't been slept in. His voice tightened. "Nothing to worry about. Obviously you've got enough to keep you busy."

"Don't be sarcastic, David. It doesn't suit you."

She took the towel from her hair and flung it aside. "If you have something to say to me, come out with it." She plucked up a comb and began to drag it through her hair.

"Do you know what you're doing?" he blurted out.

Jessica's hand paused in midstroke. Slowly she lowered the comb to place it back on the dresser. She caught a glimpse of herself—pale, shadow-eyed, damp—and inadequately covered in Slade's wrinkled shirt. "Be specific."

"You're sleeping with the writer." Shoving up his glasses, he took a step toward her.

"And if I am?" she countered tightly. "Why should you object?"

"What do you know about him?" David demanded with such sudden heat that she was rendered speechless. "He comes out of nowhere, probably without two nickels to rub together. It's a nice setup here, big house, free meals, a willing woman."

"Be careful, David." She stiffened as the anger in her eyes met his.

"How do you know he's not just a sponge? A couple million dollars is a hell of a target."

The angry color paled with hurt. "And, of course, what else could he be interested in, other than my money."

When she would have turned away, he took her shoulders. "Come on, Jessie." The eyes behind the glasses softened. "You know I didn't mean it that way. But he's a stranger and you're . . . well, you're just too trusting."

"Am I, David?" She swallowed the sudden rise of

tears as she studied his well-known face. "Have I made a mistake by trusting?"

"I don't want you to get hurt." He squeezed her shoulders before he dropped his hands. "You know I love you." The admission seemed to make him uncomfortable. With a shrug, he stuck his hands in his pockets. "And damn it, Jessica, you must know how crazy Michael is about you. He's been in love with you for years."

"But I'm not in love with him," she said quietly. "I'm in love with Slade."

"In love with him! *Jeez,* Jessie, you hardly know the guy."

The use of the silly exclamation brought a quick laugh from her as she dragged a hand through her hair. "Oh, David, I know him better than you think."

"Look, let me check into him a little bit, maybe find out—"

"No!" Swiftly, Jessica cut him off. "No, David, I won't permit that. Slade is my business."

"So was that creep from Madison Avenue who soaked you for ten thousand," he muttered.

Turning away, she covered her face with her hands. It was funny, she thought. She should be able to laugh. Two of the most important people in her life were warning her about each other.

"Hey, Jessica, I'm sorry." Awkwardly, David patted her wet hair. "That was a dumb thing to say. I'll butt out, just . . . well, just be careful, okay?" He shifted from one foot to the other, wondering why she was suddenly so emotional. "You're not going to cry or anything, are you?"

"No." That did nudge a small laugh from her. He sounded suspiciously as he had when he'd been twelve and she'd come home after fighting with her current boyfriend. Loyalty came full circle, overlapping everything else. "David . . ." Turning, Jessica laid her hands on his shoulders, looking beyond the lenses and deep into his eyes. "If you were in trouble—if you'd gotten in over your head and made a mistake, a serious one—would you tell me?"

His eyes narrowed slightly, but she couldn't tell if it was from curiosity or guilt. "I don't know. I guess it would depend."

"It wouldn't matter what you'd done, David, I'd always be on your side."

The tone was too serious. Uncomfortable, he shrugged his thin shoulders and tried to lighten it. "I'm going to remind you of that the next time you jump me for making a mistake in the books. Jessie, you really don't look good. You ought to think about getting away for a few days."

"I'll be fine." Sensing an argument, she continued. "But I'll give it some thought."

"Good. I've got to go, I told Michael I'd open up today." He gave her a quick kiss on the cheek. "I'm sorry if I came on too strong before. I still think . . ." Hesitating, he shifted his shoulders again. "Well, we've all got to do things our own way."

"Yes," she murmured as she watched him walk to the door. "Yes, we do. David . . . if you or Michael need money . . ."

"Are we going to get a raise?" he asked with a quick grin as he turned the knob.

Forcing a smile, Jessica picked up her comb again. "We'll see about it when I come back to work."

"Hurry back," he said, then left her alone.

Jessica stared at the closed door, then down at the comb in her hand. On a sudden spurt of rage, she hurled it across the room. Look at what she'd been doing! Pumping him, half hoping he'd confess so that she could see an end to things. She'd watched him, searching for some sign of guilt. And she wouldn't be able to prevent herself from doing the same with Michael. Her own lack of trust appalled her.

Dropping onto the stool of her vanity, she stared at her reflection. It wasn't right that she should feel this way—alienated from the two people she'd felt closest to. Watching for signs, waiting for them to make a mistake. Worse, she thought, worse, wanting them to make one so that she could stop the watching and waiting.

She took a long, hard look at herself. Her hair was wet and tangled around an unnaturally pale face. The pallor only accented the smudges under her eyes. She looked frail, already half beaten. That she could put an end to with a few basic practicalities. Stiffening her spine, Jessica began to dab makeup on the smudges. If an illusion of strength was all she had left, she'd make the best of it.

When the phone rang across the room, she jolted, knocking a small china vase to the floor. Helplessly, she stared at the shattered pieces that could never be put back together.

Betsy answered the phone as Slade reached the bottom of the stairs. "Yes, he's here. May I say who's calling?" She stopped Slade with an arch look as she held out the receiver. "It's a *Mrs.* Sladerman," she said primly.

Frowning, Slade took the receiver. "Mom?" Betsy sniffed at that and walked away. "Why are you calling me here? You know I'm working. Is anything wrong?" he demanded as annoyance turned to concern. "Is Janice all right?"

"Nothing's wrong and Janice is fine," his mother put in the moment he let her speak. "And how are you?"

Annoyance returned swiftly. "Mom, you know you're not supposed to call when I'm working unless it's important. If the plumbing's gone again, just call the super."

"I could probably have figured that one out all by myself," Mrs. Sladerman considered.

"Look, I should be home in a couple of days. Just put whatever it is on hold until I get there."

"All right," she said mildly. "But you did tell me to let you know if I heard anything from your agent. We'll talk about it when you get home. Good-bye, Slade."

"Wait a minute." Letting out an impatient breath, he shifted the phone to his other hand. "You didn't have to call to pass on another rejection."

"No," she agreed. "But I thought maybe I should call with an acceptance."

He started to speak, then stopped himself. Anticipation only led to disappointment. "On the new short story for *Mirror?*"

"Now, he did mention something about that

too . . ." She let the sentence trail off until Slade was ready to shout at her. "But he was so excited about selling the novel that I didn't take it all in."

Slade felt the blood pounding in his ears. "What novel?"

"Your novel, idiot," she said with a laugh. *"Second Chance* by James Sladerman, soon to be published by Fullbright and Company."

Emotion raced through him too swiftly. Resting his forehead against the receiver, he closed his eyes. He'd waited all of his life for this one moment; now nothing seemed ready to function. He tried to speak, found his throat closed, then cleared it.

"Are you sure?"

"Am I sure," she muttered. "Slade, do you think I can't understand English, even if it's fancy agent talk? He said they're working up a contract and he'll be in touch with the details. Business about film rights and serial rights and clauses with numbers. Of course," she added when her son remained silent, "it's up to you. If you don't *want* the fifty-thousand-dollar advance . . ." She waited, then gave a maternal sigh. "You always were a quiet one, Slade, but this is ridiculous. Doesn't a man say something when he finally has what he's always wanted?"

Always wanted, he thought numbly. Of course she'd known. How could he have ever deceived himself into thinking he'd concealed it from her. The money hadn't sunk in. He was still hearing the magic word *published.* "I can't think," he said finally.

"Well, when you can, get the one you're working on now together. They want to see it. Seems they think they've got a tiger by the tail. Slade . . . I wonder if I've told you often enough that I'm proud of you."

"Yeah." He let out a long breath. "You have. Thanks."

Her chuckle was warm in his ear. "That's right, darling, save your words for your stories. I have a few hundred phone calls to make now; I love to brag. Congratulations."

"Thanks," he said again, inadequately. "Mom . . ."

"Yes?"

"Buy a new piano."

She laughed. "Good-bye, Slade."

He listened to the dial tone for nearly a full minute.

"Excuse me, Mr. Sladerman, would you like your breakfast now?"

Confused, Slade turned to stare at Betsy. She stood behind him—little black eyes, wrinkled skin, and graying hair on short sturdy legs. She smelled faintly of silver polish and lavender sachet. The smile Slade gave her had her taking a cautious step back. It looked a bit crazed.

"You're beautiful."

She backed up another step. "Sir?"

"Absolutely beautiful." Swooping her up, he spun her in a fast circle, then kissed her full on the mouth. Betsy managed one muffled shriek. Her lips tingled for the first time in ten years.

"Put me down and behave yourself," she ordered, clinging to her dignity.

"Betsy, I'm crazy about you."

"Crazy, period," she corrected, refusing to be charmed by the gleam in his eye. "Just like a writer to be nipping at the brandy before breakfast. Put me down and I'll fix you some nice black coffee."

"I'm a writer," he told her with something like wonder in his voice.

"Yes, indeed," she said soothingly. "Put me down like a good boy."

Jessica stopped halfway down the steps to stare. Was that Slade grinning like a madman and holding her housekeeper two feet off the ground? Her mouth dropped open as he planted another kiss on Betsy's staunch, unpainted lips.

"Slade?"

Taking Betsy with him, he turned. It flashed through Jessica's mind that it was the first time she had seen him fully, completely happy. "You're next," he announced as he set Betsy back on her feet.

"Pixilated," Betsy told Jessica with a knowing nod. "Before breakfast."

"Published," Slade corrected as he swung Jessica from the stairs. "Before breakfast." His mouth crushed hers before she had a chance to speak. She felt the emotion coming from him in sparks; hard, clean emotion without eddies or undercurrents. The joy transferred into her so that she was laughing even as her mouth was freed.

"Published? Your novel? When? How?"

"Yes. Yes." He kissed her again before continuing to answer her questions in turn. "I just got a call. Fullbright and Company accepted my manuscript and want to see the one I'm working on." Something changed in his eyes as he drew her back against him. She saw it only briefly. It wasn't a loss of happiness, but a full dawning of realization. "My life's my own," he murmured. "It's finally mine."

"Oh, Slade." Jessica clung to him, needing to share the moment. "I'm so happy for you." Lifting her face, she framed his in her hands. "It's just the beginning. Nothing will stop you now, I can feel it. Betsy, we need champagne," she said as she wrapped her arms around Slade's neck again.

"At nine o'clock in the morning?" The sentence trembled with righteous shock.

"We need champagne at nine o'clock on *this* morning," Jessica told her. "Right away in the parlor. We're celebrating."

With her tongue clucking rapidly, Betsy moved down the hall. Writers, she reminded herself, were hardly better than artists. And everyone knew the sort of lives *they* led. Still, he was a charming devil. She allowed herself one undignified chuckle before she went into the kitchen to report the goings-on to the cook.

"Come inside," Jessica ordered. "Tell me everything."

"That's everything," Slade told her as she pulled him into the parlor. "They want the book, that's the important thing. I'll have to get the details from my agent." The figure of fifty thousand finally registered fully. "I'll get an advance," he added with a half laugh. "Enough to keep me going until I sell the second one."

"That won't be long—I read it, remember?" On a sudden burst of energy, she grabbed his hand. "What a movie it would make! Think of it, Slade, you could do the screenplay. You'll have to be careful with the film rights, make sure you don't sign away something you shouldn't. Or a miniseries," she decided. "Yes, that's better, then you could—"

"Ever thought about giving up antiques and opening an agency?" he asked mildly.

"Negotiating's negotiating," she countered, then smiled. "And I'm an artist."

With her face set in lines of disapproval, Betsy entered carrying a tray. "Will there be anything else, Miss Winslow?"

When Betsy used such formal address, Jessica knew she had sunk beyond reproach. "No, nothing, thank you, Betsy." She waited until the housekeeper had disappeared before casting Slade a baleful glance. "That's your fault really," she informed him. "She'll be polite and long-suffering all day now because you molested her and I joined you in champagne depravity before breakfast."

"We could ask her to have a glass," he suggested as he worked the cork from the bottle.

"You really do want me to be in trouble." Jessica lifted both glasses as the cork popped out. "To writing 'James Sladerman' on one of those necessary cards in my library," she said when both glasses were full.

Laughing, he clinked his rim against hers. "You'll have the first copy," he promised, then drained his glass.

"How do you feel, Slade?" Sipping more cautiously, Jessica watched him refill his glass. "How do you feel really?"

He studied the bubbles in the wine as if searching for the word. "Free," he said quietly. "I feel free."

Shaking his head, he began to wander the room. "After all these years of doing what I had to, I'll have the chance to do what I want to. The money just means that I won't starve doing it even after this last year's tuition is paid. But now the door's open. It's open," he repeated, "and I can walk through it."

Jessica moistened her lips and swallowed. "You'll quit the force now?"

"I intended to next year." He toyed with the wick of a candle on the piano. A restlessness crept into the other feelings—a restlessness he hadn't permitted himself to acknowledge before. "This means it can be sooner—much sooner. I'll be a civilian."

She thought of the gun he secreted somewhere in his rooms upstairs. Relief flowed through her to be immediately followed by anxiety. "I guess it'll take some getting used to."

"I'll manage."

"You'll . . . resign right away?"

"No need to wait," he considered. "I've got enough to get by on until the contract's signed. I'll need time if they want rewrites. Then there's this novel to finish and another I've been kicking around. I wonder how it'll feel to write full-time instead of grabbing snatches."

"It's what you were meant to do," she murmured.

"As soon as this is over, I'm going to find out."

"Over?" Her eyes fixed on his, but he wasn't looking at her. "You're staying?"

"What?" Distracted, he brought his gaze back to her. The expression on her face made him frown. "What did you say?"

"I thought you'd turn over the assignment to someone else." Jessica reached for the bottle to add champagne to a glass that was already full. "You'll want to get back to New York right away."

With deliberate care, Slade set down his glass. "I don't leave things until they're finished."

"No." She set the bottle back down. "No, of course you wouldn't."

"You think I'd walk out of here and leave you?"

The anger in his voice had her taking a quick sip of champagne. "I think," she said slowly, "when someone's about to get what they've worked for, waited for, they shouldn't take any chances."

He went to her and took the glass from her hand, then set it beside the half-filled bottle. "I think you should shut the hell up." When she started to speak, he cupped her face in one strong hand. "I mean it, Jess."

"You're a fool to stay when you have a choice," she blurted out.

His eyes narrowed with temper before he brought his mouth to hers for one brief, hard kiss. "You're a fool to think I have one."

"But you do," Jessica corrected more calmly. "I told you once before, we always have a choice."

"All right." Slade nodded, never taking his eyes off hers. "Say the word and I'll go back to New York today . . . if you'll go with me," he added when she started to speak. Her answer was a quick, defiant shake of the head. "Then we're in this together until the finish."

Jessica went into his arms and clung. She needed him to stay as badly as she wanted him to go. For now, she would only think of tomorrows. "Just remember,

I gave you your chance. You won't get another one." Tilting her head back, she smiled at him. "One day I'm going to remind you of it. We're in this together."

He nodded again, not noting that she had edited his phrase. "Okay, let's get some breakfast to go with this champagne before Betsy completely writes you off."

Chapter 10

FOR JESSICA, THE DAY CRAWLED. THE CONFINEMENT alone would have been torture to her. She hated seeing the sun pour through the windows while she remained trapped inside. Even the beach was off limits, so she was prevented from learning if she could walk there again without looking over her shoulder.

Thinking of her shop only brought on a dull, nagging headache. The one thing she'd conceived and built by herself had been taken out of her hands. Perhaps she would never feel the same pride in it, the same dedication to making it the best she was capable of. Worse, her own weariness was taking her to the point where she no longer cared.

Jessica detested being ill. Her usual defense against a physical weakness was to ignore it and go on. It was something she couldn't—or wouldn't—change. Now, however, she had no outlet. The quiet library and monotonous tasks Slade gave her were grating on already taut nerves. Finally she tossed her pen across the table and sprang up.

"I can't stand this anymore!" She gestured widely to encompass the library at large. "Slade, if I write one more word, I'll go crazy. Isn't there something we can do? *Anything?* This waiting is unbearable."

Slade leaned back in his chair, listening calmly to her complaints. He'd watched her fidget throughout the morning, fighting off boredom, tension, and exhaustion. The only surprise he felt was that she'd managed to go so long without exploding. Sitting still, he mused, was not Jess Winslow's forte. He pushed aside a pile of books.

"Gin," he stated mildly.

Jessica plunged her hands into the pockets of her trousers. "Damn it, Slade, I don't want a drink. I need to *do* something."

"Rummy," he finished as he rose.

"Rummy?" For a moment she looked puzzled, then gave a gusty sigh. *"Cards?* I'm ready to beat my head against the wall and you want to play cards?"

"Yeah. Got any?"

"I suppose." Jessica dragged a hand through her hair, holding it back from her face a moment before she dropped her arm to her side. "Is that the best you can come up with?"

"No." Slade came to her to run his thumb along the shadows under her eyes. "But I think we've given Betsy enough shocks for today."

With a half laugh, Jessica gave in. "All right then,

cards." She went to a table and pulled open a drawer. "What stakes?" she asked as she rummaged around in the drawer.

"Your capital's a bit bigger than mine," Slade said dryly. "Half a penny a point."

"Okay, big spender." Jessica located a pack of cards, then flourished them. "Prepare to lose."

And he did—resoundingly. At Slade's suggestion, they had settled in the parlor. His thoughts had been that the sofa and a quiet fire would relax her, and a steady, boring game might put her to sleep. He'd already concluded that asleep was the only way Jessica could handle the waiting without losing her mind.

He hadn't expected her to know a great deal about the game, any more than he had expected to be trounced.

"Gin," Jessica announced again.

He looked down in disgust at the cards she spread. "I've never seen anyone with that kind of luck."

"Skill," she corrected, picking up the cards to shuffle them.

His opinion was a brief four-letter word. "I've worked vice," he told her while she dealt. "I know a hustle when I see one."

"Vice?" Jessica poked her tongue in her cheek. "I'm sure that was very interesting."

"It had its moments," he muttered, scowling at the cards she'd dealt him.

"What department are you with now?"

"Homicide."

"Oh." She swallowed, but managed to keep her voice light. "I suppose that has its moments too."

He gave her a grunt that might have been agreement as he discarded. Jessica plucked it up and slipped it into her own hand. When Slade narrowed his eyes, she only smiled.

"You must have met a lot of people in your work." She contemplated her hand, then tossed out a card. "That's why your characters have such depth."

Briefly he thought of the street people; dealers and prostitutes, petty thieves and victims. Still, she was right in her way. By the time he'd hit thirty, Slade had thought he'd seen all there was to see. He was constantly finding out there was more.

"Yeah, I meet a lot of people." He discarded again, and again Jessica plucked it up. "Busted a few professional card sharks."

Jessica sent him an innocent look. "Really?"

"One was a great-looking redhead," he improvised. "Ran a portable game in some of the best hotels in New York. Soft southern accent, white hands, and a marked deck." Experimentally, he held a card to the light before he discarded it. "She went up for three years."

"Is that so?" Jessica shook her head as she reached for the card. "Gin."

"Come on, Jess, there's no way—"

Apologetically, she spread her cards. "There seems to be."

After a quick scan of her cards, he swore. "Okay, that's it." Slade tossed in his hand. "Figure up my losses. I'm finished."

"Well, let's see." Jessica chewed on the end of a pencil as she scanned the notepad dotted with numbers from previous hands. "You got caught with a bundle that time, didn't you?" Not bothering to wait for his reply, she scribbled on the pad. "The way I figure it, you owe me eight dollars and fifty-seven and a half cents." Setting down the pad, she smiled at him. "Let's just make it eight dollars and fifty seven, even."

"You're all heart, Jess."

"Just pay up." She held out a hand, palm up. "Unless you want to go for double or nothing."

"Not a chance." Slade reached into his pocket and drew out his wallet. He tossed a ten onto the table. "I haven't got any change. You owe me a buck forty-three."

With a smirk, Jessica rose to retrieve her purse from the hall closet. "One dollar," she said, rummaging through her billfold as she came back into the parlor. "And . . . twenty-five, thirty, forty-three." She dropped the change into his hand, then grinned. "We're even."

"Not by a long shot." Slade grabbed her and gave her a long, thorough kiss. "If you're going to fleece me," he murmured, gathering her hair in one hand, "the least you can do is make it worth my while."

"Seems reasonable," she agreed as she offered her lips again.

God, how he wanted her. Not just for a moment or a day or a year, he thought as he lost himself in the taste of her. For always. Forever. All those terms he never allowed himself to think. There was a wall between them—the thin glass wall of status he forgot when she was in his arms. He had no business feeling what he felt or asking what he wanted to ask. But she was warm and soft, and her lips moved willingly under his.

"Jess—"

"Don't talk." She wrapped her arms tighter around him. "Just kiss me again." Her mouth clung to his, smothering the words that begged to be said. And the longer the kiss went on, the thinner the wall between them became. Slade thought he could feel it crack, then shatter without a sound.

"Jess," he murmured again as he buried his face in her hair. "I want—"

She jolted and Slade swore when the doorbell rang.

"I'll get it," she said.

"No, let Betsy." He held her another minute, feeling the hammer of her heart against his chest.

More than willing, Jessica nodded. When Slade released her, she sank into a chair. "It's silly," she began, then Michael walked into the parlor.

"Jessica." Ignoring Slade, Michael went to her to take her hand. "You're so pale—you should be in bed."

She smiled, but couldn't prevent her fingers from tightening on his. "You know I'd go crazy if I stayed in bed. I told you not to worry, Michael."

"How could I help it?" He lifted her hand to brush his fingers over the knuckles. "Especially with David muttering all afternoon about you not knowing how to take care of yourself."

"That was—" She broke off, casting a quick look at Slade. "That was just a small disagreement we had. I'm fine, really."

"You don't look fine, you look exhausted." Frowning, Michael followed the direction of her gaze until he too looked at Slade. Understanding was followed by anger, resentment, then weary acceptance. "She should be in bed," he told Slade curtly, "not entertaining guests."

Slade shrugged as he eased himself into a chair. "It's not my place to tell Jess how to run her life."

"And what exactly is your place?"

"Michael, please." Jessica cut off Slade's answer and rose hastily. "I'll be going up soon, I am tired." With a silent plea, she turned to Slade. "I've kept you from your work too long. You haven't written all day."

"No problem." He pulled out a cigarette. "I'll make it up this evening."

Michael stood between them, obviously not wanting to leave—and knowing there was no point in staying. "I'll go now," he said at length, "if you promise to go up to bed."

"Yes, I will. Michael . . ." She put her arms around him, feeling the familiar trim build, smelling the light, sea-breeze scent of his after-shave. "You and David mean so much to me. I wish I could tell you."

"David and I," he said quietly and brushed a hand down her hair. "Yes, I know." He cast Slade a last look before he drew her away. "Good night, Jessica."

"Good night, Michael."

Slade waited until he heard the front door close. "What kind of disagreement did you have with David?"

"It was nothing to do with this—it was personal."

"Nothing's personal right now."

"This was." Turning, she fixed him with weary eyes,

but he saw the stubborn crease between her brows. "I have a right to some privacy, Slade."

"I told you not to see either of them alone," he reminded her.

"Book me," she snapped.

"Don't tempt me." He met her angry eyes directly. "And don't do it again."

"Yes, Sergeant." On a disgusted sigh, Jessica dragged a hand through her hair. "I'm sorry."

"Don't apologize," he told her briefly. "Just do what you're told."

"I think I will go up. I'm tired," she added, not looking at Slade.

"Good." He didn't get up, nor did he take his eyes off her. "Get some sleep."

"Yes, yes, I will. Good night, Slade."

He listened to her go up the steps, then tossed his cigarette into the fire and swore.

Upstairs, Jessica filled the tub. That was what she needed, she told herself—an aspirin for the headache, a hot tub for the tension. Then she would sleep. She had to sleep—her body was crying for it. For the first time in her life Jessica felt the near weightlessness of true exhaustion. She waited until the bathroom was steamy, then lowered herself into the tub.

She knew she hadn't deceived Slade. Jessica wasn't fool enough to believe that he'd taken her excuse of being tired at face value. He was just as cognizant of what was going on inside her head as she was. The visit from Michael had been the last straw in a day filled with unspoken fears and rippling tension.

Nothing had happened, she thought in frustration

as she let the water lap over her. How much longer would she have to wait? Another day? A week? Two weeks? On a long, quiet sigh she shut her eyes. Jessica understood her own personality too well. She would be lucky to get through the night much less another week of waiting and wondering.

Take an hour at a time, she advised herself. It was seven o'clock. She'd concentrate on getting through until eight.

At twenty past eight Slade went systematically through the first floor, checking locks. He'd waited, throughout an unbearably long day, for the phone call that would tell him his assignment was over. Silently he cursed Interpol, the FBI, and Dodson. As far as he was concerned, they were all equally to blame. Jessica wouldn't be able to take much more—that had been made abundantly clear during Michael's visit.

Another thing had been made abundantly clear. Slade had found himself entirely too close to stepping over the last boundary. If the doorbell hadn't rung, he would have said things best left unsaid, asked things he had no right to ask of a vulnerable woman.

She might have said yes. Would have said yes, he corrected as he stepped past a snoring Ulysses. And would have regretted it, he reflected, when the situation changed and her life was back to normal. What if he had asked her, then they'd been married before she'd had time to readjust? A good way to mess up two lives, Slade, he told himself. It was better to make the break now, draw back until they were just cop and assignment again.

At least she was upstairs resting, not beside him, tempting him to cross the line again. When she wasn't there where he could see her, touch her, it was easier to keep things in perspective.

The servants were settled in their wing. He could hear the low murmur of a television and the settling of boards. After he'd finished checking the locks, he'd go upstairs and write. Slade rubbed a hand over the back of his neck where the tension concentrated. Then he'd sleep in his own bed, alone.

As he walked toward the kitchen door, Slade saw the knob slowly turn. Muscles tensed, he stepped back into the shadows and waited.

Eight thirty. Jessica glanced at the clock again as she roamed her bedroom. Neither the bath nor the aspirin had relaxed her enough to bring sleep any closer. If Slade would come up, she thought, then shook her head. She was becoming too dependent, and that wasn't like her. Still, she felt that her nerves would calm somewhat if she could just hear the sound of his typewriter.

An hour at a time, she reminded herself, glancing at the clock yet again. Well, she'd made it from seven to eight, but she wasn't going to make it until nine. Giving up, Jessica started back downstairs.

If he's annoyed, she mused, she'd just have to make the best of it. Being confined in the house was bad enough without restricting herself to her rooms. She'd almost be willing to fill out some more of those silly cards—anything to keep her hands busy until . . .

Her thoughts broke off as she came to the foot of

the stairs. For the second time the parlor doors were closed. A tremor ran up her back, urging her to turn around, go to her room, and pretend she'd never left it. She'd taken the first step in retreat before she stopped herself.

Hadn't she told Slade not to tell her to run? This was her home, Jessica reminded herself as she stepped forward. Whatever happened in it was hers to deal with. Taking a deep breath, she opened the parlor doors and flicked on the light switch.

Slade waited as the rear door opened quietly. At first there was only a shadow, but the build was familiar. Relaxing, he stepped forward into the moonlight. Startled, David whirled around and swore.

"You scared the hell out of me," David complained as he let the door swing shut behind him. "What're you doing standing around in the dark?"

"Just checking the locks," Slade said easily.

"Moving right in," David muttered. After turning on the lights, he went over to the stove. "Want some coffee?" he asked grudgingly.

"Thanks." Slade straddled a chair and waited for David to come out with whatever was on his mind.

The last report Slade had received from Brewster had put David in the clear. His name and face and fingerprints had been run through the most sophisticated computers. His every movement had been under surveillance for over a month. David Ryce was exactly what he seemed—a young, faintly defiant man who had a knack for figures and an affection for antiques. He was also having what he thought was a discreet affair with a pre-med student. Slade recalled Brewster's almost paternal amusement with David's infatuation.

Though he'd felt an initial twinge of guilt at keeping the knowledge of David's clean slate from Jessica, Slade had decided she had enough trouble keeping herself under control. Better that she suspected both men than for her to be certain that Michael Adams was up to his neck in the smuggling operation.

"Michael." Jessica stared, facing the truth and not wanting to believe it.

"Jessica." He stood with pieces of the desk in his hand, frantically searching for some viable excuse for his presence and his actions. "I didn't want to disturb you. I'd hoped you'd be asleep."

"Yes, I'm sure you did." With a quiet, resigned sigh, she shut the parlor doors at her back.

"There was a problem with this piece," Michael began. "I wanted to—"

"Please don't." Jessica crossed the room, poured two fingers of brandy, and drank it down. "I know about the smuggling, Michael," she told him in a flat voice. "I know you've been using the shop."

"Smuggling? Really, Jessica—"

"I said don't!" She whirled sharply, pushed by anger and despair. "I *know*, Michael. And so do the police."

"Oh God." As his color drained, he looked around wildly. Was there anyplace left to run?

"I want to know why." Her voice was low and steady. "You owe me that."

"I was trapped." He let the pieces of the desk fall to the floor, then groped for a cigarette. "Jessica, I was trapped. He promised you wouldn't be involved—that you'd never have to know. You have to believe that I'd never have gotten you mixed up in this if there'd been any choice."

"Choice," she murmured, thinking of Slade. "We all have our choices, Michael. What was yours?"

"In Europe a couple of years ago, I . . ." He took a greedy drag of his cigarette. "I lost some money . . . a lot of money. More than I had to lose, and to the wrong person." He sent her a swift, pleading look. "He had me worked over—you might remember when I took those extra two weeks in Rome." He drew in and expelled smoke quickly. "They were pros. . . . It was days before I could walk. When he gave me an alternative to crippling me permanently, I took it."

Dragging a hand through his hair, Michael walked over to the bar. He poured bourbon neat, splattering drops, then downed it in one swallow. "He knew who I was, of course, my family, my connection with your shop—your unimpeachable reputation." The liquor gave him temporary strength. His voice steadied. "It worked beautifully for him. It wasn't for the money, Jessica, I just wanted to stay alive. And then . . . I was in too deep."

She felt something soften inside her and quickly pushed it aside. No pity, she ordered herself. He wouldn't drag pity from her now. "Who is *he*, Michael?"

"No." Shaking his head, he turned to face her. "I

won't tell you that. If he found out you had his name, you'd never be safe."

"*Safe?*" She laughed shortly. "If you were concerned for my safety, you might have told me not to walk on the beach when someone was going to shoot at me."

"Sh-shoot . . . good God, Jessica, I didn't think he'd. . . . He threatened, but I never believed he'd actually try to hurt you. I would have done something." His hand trembled, spilling ash onto the carpet. With a jerky movement of his arm, Michael tossed the cigarette into the fire. "I begged him not to involve you, swore I'd do anything he wanted if he'd leave you out of it. I love you, Jessica."

"Don't talk about loving to me." With more control than she was feeling, Jessica bent over to pick up one of the pieces he had dropped. It was part of the inner molding. "What's in the desk, Michael?"

"Diamonds," he said and swallowed. "A quarter of a million. If I don't take them to him tonight—"

"Where?" she interrupted.

"To the shop, ten o'clock."

"Let me see them."

She watched him separate one of the partitions of a cubbyhole from the space where a drawer had been. Lifting a thin piece of wood, he revealed a false bottom. He drew out a small padded bag. "It's the last time," he began, clutching the bag in his palm. "I've already told him I'm through. As soon as I deliver these, I'm going to leave the country."

"It is the last time," Jessica agreed, then held out her hand. "But you're not delivering anything. I'm taking the diamonds, Michael. They're going back where they came from, and you're going to the police."

"You might as well hold a gun to my head!" He swiped an unsteady hand over his mouth. "He'll kill me, Jessica. If he finds out I went to the police, I wouldn't even be safe in a cell. He'll kill me, and if he knows what you've done, he'll kill you too."

"Don't be a fool." Eyes glittering, she grabbed the bag from his hand. "He'll kill you anyway, and me. Is he stupid enough not to know the police are closing in?" she demanded. "Is he stupid enough to leave you alive as a liability? Think!" she ordered impatiently. "Your only chance is with the police, Michael."

Her words touched off a fear he'd buried. Deep inside his mind, Michael had always known his involvement in the operation could only end one way. That fear, much more than money, had kept him loyal. "Not the police." Again, his eyes darted around the room. "I have to get away. Don't you see, Jessica, someplace where he won't find me! Let me have the diamonds, I can use them."

"No." Her hand tightened on the bag. "You used me, no more."

"For God's sake, Jessica, do you want to see me dead?" His breathing was raw and jerky as the words tumbled out. "I don't have time to raise the money I'll need. If I leave now, I'll have a start."

She stared at him. A thin film of sweat covered his face, beading over lips that trembled. His eyes were glazed with terror. He'd used her, she thought, but that didn't kill the feelings she had for him. If he was determined to run, she'd give him what he wanted. Jessica crossed to a painting of a French landscape and swung it out on hidden hinges, revealing a wall safe. Quickly she twirled the tumblers and opened it.

"Take this." She offered Michael a stack of bills. "It's not worth what the diamonds are, but cash should be safer in any case. It won't take you far enough, Michael," she said quietly as he reached for the money. "But you have to make your own decision."

"There's only one I can make." He slipped the bills inside his jacket, then finally met her eyes. "I'm sorry, Jessica."

Nodding, she turned away. She heard his footsteps as he crossed to the doors. "Michael, was David involved in this?"

"No, David did nothing but take what he thought were routine orders." He saw everything he'd ever wanted, everything he'd ever cared about, slipping through his hands. "Jessica—"

"Just go, Michael. When you run, you have to run fast."

She listened for the click of the doors before she opened the padded bag. A cold, sparkling stream of diamonds fell into her palm. "So this is what my life's worth," she murmured. Carefully, she replaced them, then stared at the remains of the Queen Anne desk. "All for a whim," she whispered. If she hadn't had that impulse to bring the desk home then . . .

With a fierce shake of her head, Jessica broke off the thought. There were no if's. She needed to see Slade, but she needed a moment to herself first. On a sigh, she sank into a chair, letting the bag of diamonds fall into her lap.

"I guess Jessica told you about this morning." As the coffee heated on the stove, David reached for cups.

Slade lifted a brow. What was this, he wondered. "Shouldn't she have?" he countered.

"Look, I don't have anything against you—I don't even know you." David turned, tossing back the hair that fell over his brow. "But Jessie's important to me. When I saw her come out of your room this morning, I didn't like it." He measured the man across the room and knew he was outmatched. "I still don't like it."

Slade watched the eyes behind the lenses. So this was her private disagreement. Jessica had the loyalty she expected here, he mused. "I'd say you don't have to like it," Slade said slowly, "but Jess wouldn't feel that way."

Uncomfortable under the direct stare, David shifted a bit. "I don't want her to get hurt."

"Neither do I."

David frowned. Something about the way Slade said it made him believe it. "She's a soft touch."

Temper leaped into the gray eyes so quickly, David nearly backed away. When Slade spoke, the words were soft and deadly controlled. "I'm not interested in her money."

"Okay. Sorry." Relaxing a bit, David shrugged. "It's just that she's gotten stung before. She trusts everybody. She's really smart, you know—for a scatterbrain who forgets what she's doing because she's doing twenty things at once. But with people, Jessica wears blinders." The coffee began to boil over behind him. David spun around and turned off the burner. "Look, forget I said anything. She told me this morning it was none of my business, and it isn't. Except that . . . well, I love her, you know," he mumbled. "How's she feeling?"

"She'll be better soon."

"Boy, I hope so," he said fervently as he brought the coffee to the table. "I wouldn't want her to hear me say it, but I could use her at the shop. Between getting the new stock checked in and Michael's moodiness . . ." David grimaced and dumped milk into his coffee.

"Michael?" Slade prompted casually.

"Yeah, well, I guess everybody's entitled to a few temper tantrums. Michael just never seems to have a temper at all." He flashed Slade a grin. "Jessica would call it breeding."

"Maybe he has something on his mind."

David moved his shoulders absently before he drank. "Still, I haven't seen him this unraveled since the mix-up on the Chippendale cabinet last year."

"Oh?" Some wells, Slade mused, took no priming at all.

"It was my fault," David went on, "but I didn't know he'd bought it for a specific customer. We do that sometimes, but he always lets Jessie or me know. It was a beauty," David remembered. "Dark kingwood, great marquetry decoration. Mrs. Leeman bought it the minute it was uncarted. She was standing in the shop when the shipment came in, took one look, and wrote out a check. Michael got back from Europe the day we were packing it for delivery and had a fit. He said it had already been sold, that he'd had a cash advance." David took a quick sip of his coffee, discovered it was bitter, and drank again resignedly.

"The paperwork had been mislaid, I guess," he went on. "That was odd because Jessie's a fiend for keeping the invoices in order. Mrs. Leeman wasn't too pleased about the mix-up either," he recalled with a grin. "Jessie sold her a side table at cost to soothe her feathers."

"Who bought it?" Slade demanded.

"What, the cabinet?" David adjusted his glasses. "Lord, I don't know. I don't think Michael ever told me, and with the mood he was in, I didn't like to ask."

"You have the receipt?"

"Yeah, sure." Puzzled, David focused on him again. "At the shop. Why?"

"I have to go out." Slade rose swiftly and headed for the rear stairs. "Don't go anywhere until I get back."

"What are you—" David broke off as Slade disappeared upstairs. Maybe he was a nut after all, David mused as he frowned at Slade's empty chair. You're having a casual conversation with a guy and all of a sudden he's . . .

"Make sure Jess stays put," Slade ordered as he came down again. His jacket was already zipped over his revolver.

"Stays put?"

"Don't let anyone in the house." Slade paused long

enough to aim hard, direct eyes at David. "No one comes in, got it?"

Something in the eyes had David nodding without question.

Slade grabbed a napkin and scrawled a number on it. "If I'm not back in an hour, call this number. Tell the man who answers the story about the cabinet. He'll understand."

"The cabinet?" David stared dumbly at the napkin Slade thrust into his hand. "*I* don't understand."

"You don't have to, just do it." The back door slammed behind him.

"Yeah, sure," David grumbled. "Why should I understand anything?" A loony tune, he decided as he stuffed the napkin into his pocket. Maybe writers were supposed to be loony tunes. Jessica sure knew how to pick them. With a glance at his watch, he decided to check on her. Maybe the writer was a little loose upstairs, maybe not, but he'd managed to unsettle him. When David was halfway down the hall, the parlor doors opened.

"David!" Jessica closed the distance between them at a run, then launched herself into his arms.

"Hey, what gives!" He managed to struggle out of her hold and take her by the shoulders. "Is there a different strain of flu running around that affects the brain?"

"I love you, David." Close to tears, Jessica framed his face with her hands.

He flushed and shifted his weight. "Yeah, I love you too. Look, I'm sorry about this morning—"

"We'll talk about that later. There's a lot I have to tell you, but I need to see Slade first."

"He went out."

"Out?" Her fingers dug into David's thin arms. "Where?"

"I don't know." Intently, he studied her face. "Jessie, you're really sick. Let me take you upstairs."

"No, David, it's important." Her voice changed from frantic to stern—the one he always responded to. "You must have some idea where he went."

"I don't," he returned a bit indignantly. "We were sitting there talking one minute, and he was up and heading out the next."

"About what?" Impatient, Jessica gave him a quick shake. "What were you talking about?"

"Just this and that. I mentioned that Michael'd been moody—like he'd been when we'd had that mix-up on the Chippendale cabinet last year."

"The Chippendale . . ." Jessica pressed her hands to her cheeks. "Oh God, yes, of course!"

"Slade gave me some business about not letting anyone in the house and calling some number if he didn't get back in an hour. Hey, where are you going?"

Jessica had swung her purse from the newel post and was rummaging through it. "He's gone to the shop. To the shop and it's nearly ten! Where are my keys! Call—call the shop, see if he answers." In a quick move, she dumped the contents of her purse on the floor. *"Call!"* she repeated when David gaped at her.

"Okay, take it easy."

While Jessica made a frantic search through the items on the floor, David dialed the phone. "I can't find them. I can't—they're in my coat!" she remembered and dashed for the hall closet.

"He doesn't answer," David told her. "Probably hasn't had time to get there yet if that's where he was going in the first place. Which doesn't make any sense because it's closed and . . . Jessie, where are you going? He said you weren't to go out. Damn it, you forgot your coat. Will you wait a minute!"

But she was already racing down the front steps toward her car.

Chapter 11

IT TOOK SLADE ONLY A FEW MOMENTS TO PICK THE LOCK on the front door of the shop. If there was one thing he was going to see to before he left, he decided, it would be to get Jessica to a decent locksmith. A miracle she hasn't been cleaned out, he mused as he moved through the main shop into the back room. Blind luck, Slade concluded, then tossed his jacket over a chair. Moving in the dark, he passed through the kitchen into what served as an office.

There was a large mahogany desk with neat stacks of papers, a blotter with names and numbers scribbled on it, and a Tiffany lamp. Slade switched it on. He caught the boldly printed ULYSSES NEEDS FOOD on the blotter right beneath the scrawled "New mop hndl— Betsy annoyed." With a half grin, Slade shook his head. Jessica's idea of organization was beyond him.

Turning away, he walked to the file cabinet set in the rear corner.

The top drawer seemed to be her personal items. He found a receipt for a blouse she had bought two years before in a file marked INSURANCE POLICIES— SHOP. Between two file folders was a wrinkled grocery list. On a sound of annoyance, he pulled out the second drawer.

It was the other side of the coin. The files were neat, legible, and in perfect order. A quick flip through them showed Slade they were receipts for the current year, arranged chronologically, delivery bills, also current and chronological, and business correspondence. Each section was a study in organized filing. He thought of the top drawer and shook his head.

In the third drawer he found what he was looking for—receipts from the previous year. Slade drew out the first file folder and took it to the desk. Methodically, he scanned each one, beginning in January. He learned nothing else, when he had completed the first quarter's receipts, other than the fact that Jessica did a thriving business.

Slade replaced the first folder and drew out the second. Time ticked away as he examined each paper. He drew out a cigarette and worked patiently from month to month. He found it in June. *One Chippendale cabinet—kingwood with marquetry decoration.* His brow rose slightly at the price.

"Not a bad deal, I imagine," he murmured. Noting the name of the purchaser, he smiled. "Everyone makes a tidy little profit." After pocketing the receipt,

Slade reached for the phone. Brewster might find David's little story very interesting. Before he had punched two numbers, Slade heard the sound of a car pulling up outside. Swiftly he turned out the light. As he moved from the desk he drew out his gun.

Jessica sped along the winding back road that led to her shop. If she'd had an ounce of sense, she berated herself, she would have told David to call the number Slade had given him. Why hadn't she at least told him to keep calling the shop until he reached Slade?

Nervously, she glanced at her watch. *Ten o'clock.* Oh God, if only the man coming to meet Michael were late! Slade would be in the back room, she concluded, searching through the old receipts. What would the man do when he got to the shop and found Slade there instead of Michael? Jessica pressed down harder on the gas and flew around a turn.

The beams of approaching headlights blinded her. Overreacting, she swerved, skidding the left rear wheel on the shoulder of the road. Heart in her throat, she fishtailed, spun on gravel, then righted the car.

That's right, she thought with her heart pumping, wreck the car. That'll do everybody a lot of good. Cursing herself, Jessica wiped a damp palm on her slacks. Don't think, she ordered herself. Just drive— it's less than a mile now. Even as she said it, the car sputtered, then bucked. Frustrated, Jessica pressed down hard on the accelerator only to have the Audi stall, then die.

"No!" Infuriated, she slammed both hands against the steering wheel. The needle on the gas gauge

stayed stubbornly on empty. How many times! she demanded. How many times had she told herself to stop and fill up? Knowing it wasn't the time for self-lectures, she slammed out of the car, leaving it in the middle of the road, lights beaming. She started to run.

Slade stood pressed behind the doorway that led to the back room. He heard the quiet click of the doorknob, then the cheery jingle of bells. He waited, listening to the soft footsteps and gentle breathing. Then there was a coldly patient sigh.

"Don't be childish, Michael. It hardly pays to hide when you leave a car out front in plain view. And you should know," he added softly, "there's no place you can hide from me."

Slade hit the overhead lights as he turned into the room. "Chambers, isn't it?" he said mildly. "With the fetish for snuffboxes." He leveled the gun. "We're closed."

With no change of expression, Chambers removed his hat. "You're the stockboy, aren't you?" He gave a wheezy chuckle. "How foolish of Michael to send you. But then, he hasn't the stomach for violence."

"I don't have that problem. Rippeon's in the morgue." When Chambers gave him a pleasantly blank look, Slade continued, "Or don't you catch the names of the pros you hire?"

"Death is an occupational hazard," Chambers said with an elegant shrug. He never bothered to glance at the gun leveled at his chest. He knew a man was the real weapon, so he watched Slade's eyes. "What has Michael promised you, Mr. . . . "

"Sergeant," Slade corrected, "Sladerman, NYPD, temporarily attached to the FBI." Slade caught the faint flicker in Chambers' eyes. "The only deal I have with Adams is a quiet . . . talk in the near future involving Jessica Winslow." The thought gave Slade a moment's grim pleasure. "Game's up, Chambers. We've had Adams under surveillance for some time, along with a few other members of your team. You were all that was missing."

"A slight miscalculation on my part," Chambers murmured as he glanced around the shop. "Normally I don't involve myself directly with any of the transports. But then, Miss Winslow has such a charming shop, I couldn't resist. A pity." He looked back at Slade again. "You don't look to be the type who'll take a bribe . . . even a lucrative one."

"You seem to be a good judge of character." Keeping the gun steady, Slade reached for the phone on the counter.

With the breath tearing in her lungs, Jessica dashed the last yards toward the shop. She could see the lights glowing behind the drawn shades. Her thoughts centered solely on Slade, she hit the door at a full run.

At a speed unexpected in a man of his bulk, Chambers grabbed her the moment she stumbled inside. His arm slid around her throat. Before fear could register, Jessica felt cold steel against her temple. Slade's forward motion stopped with a jerk.

"Put down your gun, Sergeant. It seems the game isn't quite over after all." When Slade hesitated, Chambers merely smiled. "I assure you, though the gun is small, it works very well. And at this range . . ." He trailed off delicately.

Casting a furious look into Jessica's stunned eyes, Slade let the gun drop. "Okay." He held up empty hands. "Let her go."

Chambers gave him a mild smile. "Oh, I don't think so. It seems I need an insurance policy—momentarily."

"Mr. Chambers." Jessica put a hand to the arm that was constricting her air.

"The Sergeant doesn't appreciate your timing, Miss Winslow," he said pleasantly. "However, I do, very much. This, shall we say, puts a different aspect on things."

Slade shot a quick glance at the clock on his right. By his calculations, David should be calling his contact within moments. The name of the game now was stall. "You won't have to put a bullet in her," he commented, "if you keep choking her."

"Oh, I beg your pardon." Chambers loosened his hold fractionally. The gun stayed lodged at her temple. Greedy for air, Jessica gasped it in. "A beautiful creature, isn't she?" he asked Slade. "I often wished I were twenty years younger. Such a woman looks her best on a man's arm, don't you agree?"

"Mr. Chambers, what are you doing here this time of night?" It was a weak ploy, but the best Jessica could think of. "Let me go and put that thing away."

"Oh, my dear, we all know I can't do that. I would like to for your sake," he continued as Jessica, too, shifted her eyes to the clock. *How much time do we have?* she wondered frantically.

"She could be useful to you," Slade commented. "You'll need a shield to get out of this."

"I have my . . . escape routes plotted, Sergeant." He smiled. "I always leave a back door open."

"You can't expect to get away, Mr. Chambers." Jessica's eyes met Slade's, then shifted meaningfully to the clock. "Slade must have told you that the police know everything."

"He mentioned it." Keeping his arm firm, he patted her shoulder. "You became a small weakness of mine. I enjoyed those pleasant chats we had, those pleasant cups of tea. I felt badly that this was to be my last shipment before moving on. Oh yes," he said to Slade, "I was aware the authorities were getting close, though I confess I miscalculated just how close. And though it would seem the diamonds are temporarily lost, I'll find Michael eventually."

"He doesn't have them," Jessica said quickly, then grabbed Chambers' arm as it cut off her breath again.

"No?" The word was soft and silky. Even as Slade anticipated moving forward, Chambers shot him a warning look. "Where are they?"

Jessica swallowed, straining to hear the sound of sirens. *Why don't they come!* "I'll show you." Perhaps she could bargain for Slade's life. If she could keep him alive, then get Chambers out of the shop, even for a little while . . .

"Oh no, that won't do." He tightened his grip again. "Tell me."

"No." Jessica managed to whisper the word. "I'll take you."

Without speaking, Chambers took the gun from her temple and aimed it at Slade.

"No, don't! I have them at home," she said frantically. "I have them in the wall safe in the parlor. Don't hurt him, please. I'll give you the combination. Thirty-five to the right, twelve to the left, five right, and left to twenty-three. They're all there, I wouldn't let Michael take them."

"Honest," Chambers commented. "And trusting. I am fond of you, my dear, so I suggest you close your eyes. When it comes to your turn, I promise to make it as painless as possible."

Even as Slade made his move, Jessica screamed in protest. *"No!"* Using all of her weight and the adrenaline of terror, she flung herself on the arm holding the gun. She heard the shot echoing in her head as she stumbled, then was shoved roughly aside.

Jessica landed in a heap. She felt the pain in her shoulder as it connected with the floor, tasted the iron flavor of blood or fear in her mouth as she scrambled up. As she pushed the hair out of her eyes she saw Slade's fist fly toward Chambers' face. The portly man seemed to crumble layer by layer on his way to the floor.

So quickly, she thought numbly. It was all over so quickly. One moment they were both at the edge of their lives, and then it was over. She'd never take her life for granted again—not a second of it. Weakly, she leaned back against a highboy.

"Slade . . ."

"Get me some rope or cord from the back room, you idiot."

She pressed her fingers between her brows and stifled a hysterical giggle. So much for romantic endings, she thought as she stumbled blindly toward the storeroom. Blinking away the haze that covered her eyes, Jessica found some packing cord. She stared at it a moment, losing track of why she needed it.

"Will you hurry up!" Slade shouted at her.

Responding automatically, she brought it out to him. Ten fifteen, she thought as she passed the clock. How could it only be ten fifteen? Could people come so close to death and escape all in ten minutes? Slade ripped the cord out of her hand without looking up.

"Damn it, Jess, of all the stupid things to do! What the hell do you mean by bursting in here like that? You know you weren't to leave the house." Binding the unconscious Chambers, Slade let out a steady stream of curses.

"Michael told me ten o'clock," she murmured. "And I thought—"

"If you'd had a thought in your head you would have stayed put like you were told. What did you think you could do, racing out here like this. Damn it, I had him before you came barrelling through the door. That's not even enough for you." He secured the knot, then pushed passed her on the way to the phone. "Then you throw yourself on the gun." He wrenched off the receiver and started to dial. "You could've been shot."

"Yes." In dumb fascination, Jessica stared down at the stain spreading on the arm of her sweater. "I think I was."

"What?" Annoyed, he turned back to her, then dropped the phone out of suddenly nerveless hands. "Oh my God." In two strides he was back beside her, ripping the arm of the sweater off by the seam. "Jess, you're hit!"

Brows lowered in concentration, she stared at the wound. "Yes, I am," she said in the deliberately steady voice of a drunk. "I don't feel it. Should it hurt? There's a lot of blood."

"Shut up, damn it, just shut up!" He examined the wound quickly, seeing that the bullet had gone cleanly through the flesh. *Jess's flesh*, he thought. His stomach rolled. He stripped off his shirt and tore it into a tourniquet. "Stupid fool, you're lucky it wasn't your head." His hands trembled, causing him to fumble with the knot and curse her more violently.

"It was a little gun," she managed.

He shot her a look, ripe with conflicting emotions, but her vision was blurred. "A bullet's a bullet," he muttered. Feeling the warmth of her blood on his hands, he swallowed. A line of sweat ran down his naked back. "Damn it, Jess, what were you trying to do, jumping out that way? I knew what I was doing."

"Terribly sorry." Her head lolled a bit as she tilted it back and tried to focus on him. "How rude of me to intercept a bullet with your name on it."

"Don't get cute now," he said between his teeth. "If you weren't bleeding, I swear, I'd deck you." He wanted to hold her and was terrified she'd dissolve in his arms. His throat was dry from the rawness of his own breathing as he forced himself to treat her arm as an object, not part of her. When he'd finished binding the wound, Slade held her steady with one hand. "You probably saw that move on one of your stupid movies. Is that why you threw yourself at the gun?"

"No." She felt as if she were floating as he started to lead her to a chair. "Actually, Sergeant, it was because I thought he would kill you. Since I'm in love with you, I couldn't allow that."

He stopped dead at her words and stared down at her. When he opened his mouth to speak, he found he couldn't form a sound, much less a word. His hand dropped away from her uninjured arm.

"I'm really sorry," Jessica said in a thick voice. "But I think I'm going to faint."

The last thing she heard over the buzzing in her head was a stream of curses.

Jessica floated toward consciousness to a blur of white. She felt as though her body were drifting, apart from her mind. Even the steady throb in her shoulder seemed separate from her. The white dimmed to gray, then gradually lightened again until she focused on what was a wall. Perplexed, she stared at it.

With an interest dulled by medication, she shifted her gaze. All the walls were white, she noted. There were horizontal blinds at the window that showed hints of night between their slants. The blinds were white, too, as was the bandage around the arm that didn't feel like part of her. She remembered.

Letting out a sigh, she focused on a blue plastic pitcher and a clear plastic glass. Hospital, she thought with an absent grimace. She hated hospitals. A face bent over her, obscuring her line of vision. Amber eyes studied pale blue. They were nice enough eyes, she decided, in a round smooth face with a hint of jowl. She spotted the white coat and stethoscope.

"Doctor," she said in a whispery voice that made her frown.

"Miss Winslow, how are you feeling?"

She thought about it seriously for a moment. "Like I've been shot."

He gave a pleasant chuckle as he took her pulse. "A sensible answer," he concluded. "You'll do."

"How long . . ." She moistened dry lips and tried again. "How long have I been here?"

"Just over an hour." Taking out a slim flashlight, he aimed the beam at her right eye, then her left.

"It feels like days."

"The medication makes you sluggish. Any pain?"

"Just a throb—it doesn't feel like my arm."

He smiled and patted her hand. "It's yours."

"Slade. Where's Slade?"

His brow creased, then cleared. "The sergeant? He's spent most of his time pacing the corridors like a madman. He wouldn't wait in the lounge when I ordered him to."

"He's better at giving orders." Jessica lifted her head off the pillow, letting it fall back again when the room whirled around.

"Lie still," he told her firmly. "You'll be spending a little time with us."

The line appeared between her brows. "I don't like hospitals."

He only patted her hand again. "A pity."

"Let me see Slade," she demanded in the best authoritative voice she could muster. Her eyelids threatened to droop and she forced them open. "Please," she added.

"I don't think you take orders any better than he does."

"No." She managed a smile. "I don't."

"I'll let him come in, a few minutes only." Then, he thought as he studied her eyes, you'll sleep for the next twenty-four hours.

"Thanks."

With an absent nod, he murmured something to the nurse who entered.

Slade paced up and down the hospital corridor. Dozens of thoughts, dozens of fears, raced through his mind. A headache pulsed behind his right temple. She'd been so pale—no, it was just shock, she'd be fine. She'd been unconscious through the ambulance ride. It was better that way—she might have been in pain. God, where was the doctor? If anything happened to her. . . . His stomach convulsed again. Swallowing, Slade forced the muscles to relax, turned fear to anger. The headache spread to the back of his neck. If they didn't let him see her soon, he was going to . . .

"Sergeant?"

Whirling, Slade caught the doctor by the lapel of his coat. "Jess? How is she? I want to see her now. Can I take her home?"

Well versed in dealing with frantic spouses, parents, and lovers, the doctor spoke calmly without bothering to struggle out of the hold. "She's awake," he said simply. "Why don't we sit down?"

Slade's fingers tightened. "Why?"

"Because I've been on my feet since eight o'clock this morning." With a sigh, he decided it was best to treat this one standing up. "Miss Winslow is as well as can be expected."

"What the hell does that mean?"

"Exactly what it says," the doctor returned evenly. "You did a good job of emergency first aid. As to your second question, you can see her in a moment, and no, you can't take her home. Does she have any family?"

Slade felt the color drain from his face. "Family? What do you mean family? The wound wasn't that bad, the bullet went clean through. I had her here inside a half hour."

"You did very well," the doctor told him. "I simply want to keep her here for a few days under observation. I need to know who to notify."

"Observation?" Terrifying visions ran through his mind. "What's wrong with her?"

"To put it simply, exhaustion and shock. Would you like more complicated medical terms?"

Shaking his head, Slade released him and turned away. "No." He rubbed his hands over his face. "That's all it is, then? She's going to be all right?"

"With rest and care. Now, her family?"

"There isn't anyone." For lack of something to do with his hands, Slade stuck them in his pockets. A sensation of utter helplessness covered him, sapping the strength that tension and anger had given him. "I'll take the responsibility."

"I know this is a police matter, Sergeant, but what exactly is your relationship to Miss Winslow?"

Slade gave a short laugh. "Baby sitter," he muttered. "I'll take the responsibility," he repeated with more force. "Call Commissioner Dodson, NYPD—

he'll verify it." Turning back, he fixed the doctor with a steady look. "I want to see her. Now."

Jessica was watching the door when Slade opened it. Her lips curved. "I knew you'd find a way to get past the guards. Can you bust me out of this place?"

Keeping his hands in his pockets, he crossed to her. She was as white as the sheets she lay on. Only her eyes gave a hint of color. He thought of the first day he had seen her—vibrant, rushing. A feeling of total inadequacy swept over him so that the hands in his pockets balled into fists.

"How do you feel?"

"I told the doctor I felt like I'd been shot." Gingerly, she touched the bandaged arm. "Actually I feel like I've drunk a half dozen martinis and fallen off a cliff." She sighed, closing her eyes briefly. "You're not going to get me out of here, are you?"

"No."

"I didn't think so." Resigned, she opened her eyes again to stare at the blue plastic pitcher. "Slade, I lied about the diamonds. I tossed them under the seat in my car. It's in the middle of the road on the way to the shop. I forgot to get gas." She looked at him then. "It's not even locked. And . . ." Jessica moistened her lips when he remained silent. "I gave Michael money to get away. That's accessory after the fact or something, isn't it? I suppose I'm in trouble."

"I'll take care of it."

Even through her drugged haze, she felt surprise. "Aren't you going to shout at me?"

"No."

Fighting to keep her eyes open, Jessica laughed.

"I'll have to get shot more often." She held out a hand, not noticing his hesitation to take it. "David wasn't involved. Michael told me everything. David had no idea what was going on."

"I know."

"It seems I was half right," she murmured.

"Jess . . ." Her hand felt so fragile. "I'm sorry."

"What for?" Jessica found that it took much too much effort to keep her eyes open. The world was soft and gray when she closed them. She thought she felt his fingers lace with hers but couldn't be sure. "You didn't do anything."

"No." Slade looked down at her hand. It was limp now; he had only to release it for it to fall back on the bed. "That's what I'm sorry for."

"It's all over now, isn't it, Slade?"

Her breathing was deep and even before he answered. "It's all over now, Jess." Bending, he pressed his lips to hers, then walked away.

Chapter 12

SLADE BANKED DOWN THE UNCOMFORTABLE SENSATION of déjà vu as he waited in the commissioner's outer office. His scowl was a bit more pronounced than it had been the first time he had sat there. Three weeks had passed since he had left Jessica's bedside.

He'd gone directly back to her home on leaving the hospital. There, he'd had to deal with a puzzled, then furious, then frantic David.

"Shot, what do you mean *shot!*" Slade could still visualize the pale, strained look on David's face, still hear the trembling, angry words. "If you're a cop, why didn't you protect her?"

He'd had no answer for that. Slade had gone up to pack even as David had dialed the number of the hospital. Then he'd driven home, taking the miles to New York in a numbed weariness.

Slade had told himself to cross Jessica off, as he

crossed off what he considered the final assignment in his police career. She'd get the care and the rest she needed. When she was ready to go home, the nightmare would be behind her. And so, he told himself, would he.

Then fatigue, the bone-deep exhaustion that comes after a long, intense period of tension, did the rest for him. He collapsed into bed and slept around the clock. But she had been the first thing in his mind when he woke.

He'd called the hospital daily, telling himself he was just tying up loose ends. The reports were always the same—resting comfortably. There were days when Slade had to fight the urge to get into his car and go back to her. Then she was released. He told himself that was the end of it.

Slade had plunged into an orgy of work. The novel was finished in a marathon sixteen-hour stint while he kept his door locked and his phone off the hook. With his resignation turned in, there were only a few necessary visits to the station house. More loose ends. He signed his contract and mailed his agent a copy of his second novel.

The reports and debriefings on the smuggling case brought Jessica back too vividly. Slade filled out his papers and answered questions with a brevity that bordered on curtness. He took the professional praise for his work in stony silence. He wanted it over— completed. He reminded himself that his life was his own for the first time in thirty-three years. But she wouldn't leave him alone.

She was there at night when he lay awake and restless. She was there in the afternoon when he poured his concentration into the outline of his next novel. She was there, always there, whether he walked the streets alone or surrounded himself with people.

He could see her on the beach, laughing, the wind grabbing at her hair as she tossed driftwood for the dog to chase. He could see her in the kitchen of the shop, slicing sandwiches while the sun dappled over her skin. Though he tried to block it out, he could hear the way she murmured his name when she lay in his arms, soft and warm and eager. Then he would see her white and unconscious—and her blood was on his hands.

The guilt would overwhelm him until he threw himself into work again, using the characters he developed to dilute her memory. But they all seemed to have pieces of her—a gesture, a phrase, an expression. How could he escape someone who seemed to know where he would run, how fast, and how far?

Now, sitting again in Dodson's outer office, Slade told himself this would be the end of it. He'd known all along that Dodson would want a personal meeting. Once it was done, all ties would be severed.

"Sergeant?"

He glanced up at the secretary, oblivious this time to the slow, inviting smile she sent him. Without a word, he rose to follow her into Dodson's office.

"Slade." Dodson leaned back in his chair as Slade entered, then gave his secretary a brief nod. "No calls," he ordered. "Have a seat."

Silently, Slade obeyed while the commissioner sucked pleasurably on a cigar until the tip glowed.

Smoke wafted to the ceiling in a spiraling column which Dodson watched with apparent fascination.

"So, congratulations are in order." When Slade gave him nothing but the same silent stare, Dodson continued. "On your book," he said. Absently, he fingered his small, scrolled tie pin. "We're sorry to lose you." Saying nothing, Slade waited for the pleasantries to be over. "In any event"—Dodson leaned forward to tap his cigar ash—"your last case is wrapped up, by all accounts tightly. I don't doubt we'll get a conviction. You're aware that Michael Adams has made a full confession?"

He sent Slade an arch look and got no reply. "The domino theory seems to be working very well in this case—one name leads to another. As far as Chambers himself goes, we've got enough on him to put him away. Conspiracy to commit murder, accessory to murder, attempted murder—perhaps murder one on that business in Paris—not to mention the robberies and smuggling. No . . ." Dodson regarded the tip of his cigar with interest. "I don't think we need worry about him for quite some time."

He waited for a full thirty seconds, then went on as if he were engaged in a two-way conversation. "You'll give your evidence, naturally, when the time comes, but it shouldn't interfere too much with your new career." *Stubborn young fool,* he thought as he puffed on his cigar. He decided to test the younger man's iron control by saying a name. "Jessica told me she gave Michael several thousand dollars to aid in his escape."

Watching for a reaction, he caught the faintest

flicker in Slade's eyes—here then gone. It was all he needed to confirm the notion that had seeded in his mind when he had seen his goddaughter. "She felt that made her an accessory. Strange, Michael never mentioned her giving him any money—and I spoke with him myself. There's a rumor that you saw him too, right after he was brought in. . . ." Dodson let the sentence trail off suggestively. When Slade didn't rise to the bait, Dodson went on, undaunted. He'd cracked a few tough eggs in his own career, on the street and behind a desk.

"I imagine a few choice words were sufficient to keep Michael quiet, and of course, Jessica can afford to lose a few thousand. We might have a bit of trouble keeping *her* quiet, though." He smiled. "That conscience of hers, you know."

"How is she?" The words were out before Slade could stop them. Though he swore under his breath, Dodson gave no sign of hearing.

"She's looking very well." He swiveled gently in his chair. "I'll tell you, Slade, I was shaken when I visited her in the hospital. I've never known Jessica to be ill in her life, and . . . well, it was quite a shock." Slade pulled out a cigarette, lighting a match with sharp, controlled violence. "She's bounced back," the commissioner continued, pleased with the reaction. "Drove the doctor crazy until he'd let her out, then she went right back to work.

"That shop of hers." He gave Slade a quick grin. "I don't suppose the notoriety will do her business any harm." Noting the tension in the set of Slade's shoulders, Dodson paused long enough to tap out his cigar. "She speaks very highly of you."

"Really?" Slade expelled a long stream of smoke. "My assignment was to keep her safe—I did a remarkably poor job of it."

"She is safe," Dodson corrected. "And as stubborn as ever. David and I both tried to persuade her to go to Europe, take a little time off to get her bearings. She won't hear of it." He settled back in his chair as a faint smile flickered on his lips. "Says she's going to stay put."

Slade's eyes flew from the view out the window to pin Dodson's. Emotions smoldered in them, fiercely, quickly, then were suppressed. "Hard to believe," he managed. "She never did before."

"So she tells me." Dodson steepled his fingers. "She's given me a full report—with a great many details you omitted from yours. Apparently," Dodson commented as Slade narrowed his eyes, "you had your hands full."

"Full enough," Slade returned.

Dodson pursed his lips, in speculation or agreement, Slade couldn't tell. "Jessica seems to think she handled the entire business badly."

"She handled it too well," Slade disagreed in a mutter. "If she'd fallen apart, I could have gotten her out."

"Yes, well . . . differing points of view, of course." Dodson's gaze fell on the triple-framed photos of his wife and children. He'd had a few . . . differing points of view with that lady from time to time. He remembered the look in Jessica's eyes when she'd asked for Slade. "Of course, now that it's over," he ventured, "I'm not entirely sure she won't fall apart—delayed reaction."

Slade smothered the instant urge to protect and prevent. "She'll get through the aftermath all right. There're enough people in that house to take care of her."

Dodson laughed. "That's usually the other way around. Half the time Jessica serves her staff. Of course, Betsy will cluck around her for a time until Jessica's ready to scream. And of course, Jessica won't. Betsy's been with her for twenty years. Then there's the cook, she's been there nearly as long. Makes great biscuits." He paused reminiscently. "I guess it was about three years ago that Jessica picked up all her medical bills when she had a stroke. I suppose you saw old Joe, the gardener."

Slade grunted, crushing out his cigarette. "He must be ninety years old."

"Ninety-two if memory serves me. She doesn't have the heart to let him go, so she hires a young boy during the summer to do the heavy work. The little maid, Carol, is the daughter of her father's chauffeur. Jessica took her on when the girl's father died. That's Jessica." He sighed gustily. "Loyal. Her loyalty's one of her more endearing traits and one of her most frustrating." Now, Dodson concluded, was the time to drop the bomb. "She's hired a lawyer for Michael."

This time the reaction was fast and furious. "She did *what?*"

While he lifted his hands, palms up, in a gesture of helplessness, Dodson struggled with a smile. "She tells me she feels it's her responsibility."

"Just how does she come by that?" Slade demanded. His control deserted him so that he sprang up and paced the office.

"If he hadn't been working for her, he wouldn't have gotten tangled up in this mess. . . ." Dodson shrugged. "You know how her mind works as well as I do."

"Yeah. When it works at all. Adams is the one who got her involved. He's responsible for everything that happened to her. She was nearly killed twice because he didn't have the spine to protect her."

"Yes," Dodson agreed quietly. *"He's* responsible." The emphasis on the pronoun was slight, but full of meaning. Slade turned back at that. Dodson met his eyes with a look that was too understanding and too knowledgeable. He thought Slade looked like his father for a moment—impulsive, emotional, hotheaded. But Tom, Dodson mused, would never have been able to struggle with such turbulent feelings and win. Slade turned away from him again.

"If she wants to hire a lawyer for him," he murmured, "that's her business. It's got nothing to do with me."

"No?"

"Look, Commissioner." On a spurt of fury, Slade whirled around. "I took the assignment, I finished the assignment. I've written my report and been debriefed. I've also turned in my resignation. I'm finished."

Let's see how long you can convince yourself of that, Dodson mused. Smiling, he extended his hand. "Yes, as I said, we're sorry to lose you."

The air smelled of snow when Slade climbed out of his car. He glanced up at the sky—no moon, no stars. There was a keen night wind that made low howling noises through the naked trees. He shifted his gaze to the house. Lights glowed here and there; in the parlor, in Jessica's bedroom. Even as he watched, the upstairs light winked out.

Maybe she's gone to bed, he thought, hunching his shoulders against the cold. I should go—I shouldn't even be here. Even as he told himself so, he walked up the steps to the front door. He told himself he should turn around, get back in the car, and drive away. He cursed whatever demon had prompted him to make the trip in the first place. He lifted his hand to knock.

Before Slade's fist connected with the wood, the door flew open. He heard Jessica's breezy laugh, felt the quick brush of fur against his legs, then caught her as she raced out after Ulysses and collided with his chest.

Everything, everything he had tried to forget, came back to him in that one instant—the feel of her, the scent, the taste of her skin under his lips. Then Jessica tilted back her head and looked him fully in the face.

Her eyes were bright and alive, her skin flushed with laughter. As he stood tense, her lips curved for him in a smile that made his legs weak.

"Hello, Slade. I'm sorry, we almost knocked you flat."

Her words were truer than she knew, he thought. Quickly he released her and took a step back. "You're going out?"

"Just for a run with Ulysses." Jessica looked beyond his shoulder. "And he's gone now." Looking back at Slade, Jessica offered her hand. "It's good to see you. Come in and have a drink."

Warily, Slade stepped inside, but evaded the offered hand. She turned away to fling her jacket over
the newel post, shutting her eyes tightly a moment
when her back was to him. "Let's go in the parlor,"
she said brightly when she faced him again. "There's a
nice fire in there."

Without waiting for his answer, Jessica dashed
away. She was moving, Slade observed, at her usual
speed. And the shadows were gone from under her
eyes—gone as if they had never existed. She was as
she had been in the beginning—a woman with bound-
less energy. He followed her more slowly into the
parlor. She was already pouring Scotch into a glass.

"I'm so glad you came, the house is too quiet."
Jessica picked up a decanter of vermouth with no idea
what was inside. As she poured she continued to talk.
"It was wonderful for a few days, but now I almost
regret that I sent everyone away. Of course, I had to
lie to get them out of here." You're talking too fast,
too fast, she told herself, but couldn't stop. "I told
David and the staff I was going to Jamaica to lie in the
sun for a week, then I bought them all airline tickets
and shoved them out of the house."

"You shouldn't be alone." He was frowning at her
when she handed him his drink.

"Why not?" With a laugh, Jessica tossed back her
hair. "I couldn't stand being treated like an invalid. I
got enough of that in the hospital." Sipping her drink,
she turned to the fire. She wouldn't let him see the
hurt. Every day that she'd been confined in that
sterile white room she had waited for his call, watched
the door for his visit. Nothing. He'd cut himself out of
her life when she'd been too weak to prevent it. Slade

stared at her slim, straight back and wondered how he could leave without touching her.

"How are you?" The question was curt and brief.

Jessica's fingers tightened on her glass. *Do you care?* she wondered. She sipped the vermouth, making the words slip back down her throat. Turning, she smiled at him. "How do I look?"

He stared at her until the need was a hard ball in his stomach. "You need to gain some weight."

She laughed shortly. "Thank you very much." Needing to do something, Jessica wandered over to toy with the keys of the piano. "Did you finish your book?"

"Yes."

"Then everything's going well for you?"

"Everything's going just dandy." He drank, willing the liquor to dull the ache.

"Your mother liked the figure?"

Confused, he drew his brows together. "Oh, yeah. Yeah, she liked it."

They lapsed into silence, accented by the crackling wood and drifting notes. There was too much to say, Slade thought. And nothing to say. Again, he cursed himself for not being strong enough to stay away.

"You've gone back to work?" he asked.

"Yes. We've had a stream of customers since the publicity. I suppose it'll taper off. Have you resigned from the force?"

"Yes."

Silence fell again, more thickly. Jessica stared down at the piano keys as if she were about to compose a symphony. "You'd want to tie up loose ends, wouldn't you?" she murmured. "Am I a loose end, Slade?"

"Something like that," he muttered.

Her head came up at that, and her eyes fixed on his once, searingly. Turning away, she walked to the window. "Well then," she whispered. With her finger, she drew a maze on the glass. "I think I've told every proper authority every proper thing. There was a steady stream of men in dark suits in my hospital room." She dropped her hand to her side. "Why didn't you come to see me . . . or call?" Her voice steadied as she stared at the reflection of the lamp in the window. "Shouldn't there have been a final interview for your report—or is that why you came tonight?"

"I don't know why the hell I came," he tossed back, then slammed down his empty glass. "I didn't come to see you because I didn't want to see you. I didn't call because I didn't want to talk to you."

"Well, that certainly clears that up."

He took a step toward her, stopped himself, then thrust his hands in his pockets. "How's your arm?"

"It's fine." Absently, she reached up to touch the wound that had healed while she thought of the one that hadn't. "The doctor says I won't even have a scar."

"Great. That's just great." Slade pulled out a pack of cigarettes, then tossed it on a table.

"I like the idea," Jessica returned calmly. "I'm not fond of scars."

"Did you mean what you said?" It rushed out of him before he could think to prevent it.

"About the scar?"

"No, not about the damn scar." Frustrated, he dragged a hand through his hair.

"I try to mean what I say," she murmured. Her heart was in her throat now, so that she forced herself to say each word carefully.

"You said you were in love with me." Every muscle in his body tensed. "Did you mean it?"

Taking a deep breath, Jessica turned back to him. Her face was composed, her eyes calm. "Yes, I meant it."

"It's your warped sense of gratitude," he told her, then paced to the fire and back again.

Something began to warm in her. Jessica felt simultaneous sensations of relief and amusement. "I think I could tell the difference," she considered. "Sometimes I'm very grateful to the butcher for a good cut of meat, but I haven't fallen in love with him . . . yet."

"Oh, you're funny." Slade shot her a furious glance. "Don't you see it was just circumstance, just the situation?"

"Was it?" Jessica smiled as she crossed to him. Slade backed away.

"I don't want any part of you," he told her heatedly. "I want you to understand that."

"I think I understand." She lifted a hand to his cheek. "I think I understand very well."

He caught her wrist, but couldn't force himself to toss it aside. "Do you know how I felt, having you unconscious—your blood on my hands? Do you know what it did to me, seeing you in that hospital bed? I've seen corpses with more color." She felt his fingers tremble lightly before they dropped her wrist. "Damn it, Jess," he breathed before he spun away to pour himself another drink.

"Slade." Jessica wrapped her arms around his

waist. Why hadn't she thought of that? she demanded of herself. Why hadn't she realized that he would blame himself? "I was the one who was in the wrong place at the wrong time."

"Don't." He put his hands on hers, firmly pushing them away. "I've got nothing for you, can't you understand? Nothing. Different poles, Jess. We barely speak the same language."

If he had faced her, he would have seen the line form between her brows. "I don't know what you're talking about."

"Look at this place!" He gestured around the room as he whirled to her. "Where you live, how you live. It's got nothing to do with me."

"Oh." Pursing her lips, she considered. "I see, you're a snob."

"Damn you, can't you see anything!" Infuriated, he grabbed her shoulders. "I don't want you."

"Try again," she suggested.

He opened his mouth, then relieved his frustration by shaking her. "You've no right—no right to get inside my head this way. I want you out. Once and for all I want you out!"

"Slade," she said quietly, "why don't you stop hating it so much and give in? I'm not going anywhere."

How his hands found their way into her hair, he didn't know. But they were sunk deep, and so was he. Struggling all the way, he gave in. "I love you, damn it. I'd like to choke you for it." His eyes grew dark and stormy. "You worked on me," he accused as she gazed up at him, calm and composed. "Right from the beginning you worked on me until I can't function without you. For God's sake, I could smell you down at the station house."

Pushed as much by fury as by need, he dragged her into his arms. "I thought I'd go mad unless I could taste you again." His lips covered hers, not gently. But then Jessica wasn't looking for gentleness. Here was the hard, bruising contact she had longed to feel again. Her response came in an explosion of heart, body, and mind so that her demand met his and fulminated. They clung for one long shimmering instant, then they were tangled together on the hearth rug.

"I need you." The words shuddered from him as two pairs of hands struggled with clothes. "Now." He found her naked breast and groaned. "It's been so long."

"Too long."

Words were no longer possible. Beside them the fire sizzled, new flames licking at wood. Wind rattled at the windows. They heard nothing, felt nothing, but each other. Lips sought, then devoured; hands explored, then possessed. There was no time for a slow reacquaintance. Hungry, they came together swiftly, letting sharp pleasure cleanse all doubts. They remained close, body to body and mouth to mouth, until need drifted to contentment.

Jessica held him against her when he would have shifted to her side. "No, don't move," she murmured.

"I'm crushing you."

"Only a little."

Slade lifted his head to grin at her and found himself lost in the cloudy amber of her eyes. Slowly, he traced the slanted line of her cheekbone. "I love you, Jess."

"Still angry about it?" she asked.

Before he buried his face at her throat, she caught the grin. "Resigned."

On a small gasp, she punched his shoulder. "Resigned, huh? That's very flattering. Well, let me tell you, I didn't picture myself falling in love with a bad-tempered ex-cop who tries to order me around."

That musky, woodsy fragrance of her skin distracted him. He began to nuzzle at her neck, wallowing in it. "Who did you picture yourself falling in love with?"

"A cross between Albert Schweitzer and Clark Gable," she told him.

Slade gave a snort before raising his head again. "Yeah? Well, you came close. Are you going to marry me?"

Jessica lifted a brow. "Do I have a choice?"

Bending, he nibbled on her lips. "Aren't you the one who says a person always has a choice?"

"Mmm, so I am." She pulled him closer for one long, satisfying kiss. "I suppose we both have one to make, don't we?"

Their eyes met, then they spoke together. "You."

If you enjoyed this book...

Thrill to 4 more
Silhouette Intimate Moments
novels (a $9.00 value)—
ABSOLUTELY FREE!

If you want more passionate sensual romance, then Silhouette Intimate Moments novels are for you!

In every 256-page book, you'll find romance that's electrifying...involving... and intense. And now, these larger-than-life romances can come into your home every month!

4 FREE books as your introduction.

Act now and we'll send you four thrilling Silhouette Intimate Moments novels. They're our gift to introduce you to our convenient home subscription service. Every month, we'll send you four new Silhouette Intimate Moments books. Look them over for 15 days. If you keep them, pay just $9.00 for all four. Or return them at no charge.

We'll mail your books to you *as soon as they are published.* Plus, with every shipment, you'll receive the Silhouette Books Newsletter absolutely free. *And Silhouette Intimate Moments is delivered free.*

Mail the coupon today and start receiving Silhouette Intimate Moments. Romance novels for women...not girls.

Silhouette Intimate Moments

Silhouette

Intimate Moments

more romance, more excitement

— **$2.25 each** —

Silhouette
Intimate Moments

more romance, more excitement

#40 ☐ **A TIME TO SING**
Kathryn Belmont

#41 ☐ **WIDOW WOMAN**
Parris Afton Bonds

#42 ☐ **HER OWN RULES**
Anna James

#43 ☐ **RUSSIAN ROULETTE**
Möeth Allison

#44 ☐ **LOVE ME BEFORE DAWN**
Lindsay McKenna

#45 ☐ **MORNING STAR**
Kristen James

#46 ☐ **CRYSTAL BLUE DESIRE**
Monica Barrie

#47 ☐ **WIND WHISPERS**
Barbara Faith

#48 ☐ **CRY FOR THE MOON**
Pamela Wallace

#49 ☐ **A MATTER OF CHOICE**
Nora Roberts

#50 ☐ **FORGOTTEN PROMISES**
April Thorne

#51 ☐ **ALTERNATE ARRANGEMENTS**
Kathryn Thiels

#52 ☐ **MEMORIES THAT LINGER**
Mary Lynn Baxter

SILHOUETTE INTIMATE MOMENTS, Department IM/5
1230 Avenue of the Americas
New York, NY 10020

Please send me the books I have checked above. I am enclosing
$_____ (please add 75¢ to cover postage and handling. NYS and
NYC residents please add appropriate sales tax). Send check or money
order—no cash or C.O.D.'s please. Allow six weeks for delivery.

NAME_____

ADDRESS_____

CITY_____STATE/ZIP_____

Silhouette Intimate Moments

Coming Next Month

Objections Overruled by Pat Wallace

Kaiti and Tor had once been husband and wife but the time hadn't been right for their love. Now they were together once more—as opposing lawyers in a murder trial. Kaiti knew she could save her client but could she defend her heart against Tor?

Seize The Moment by Ann Major

Threats on her life drove top model Andrea Ford to Mexico, only to find that love had failed her. There she met courageous painter Race Jordan, but did she dare try to find *real* love—and safety—with the brother of the man who had betrayed her?

Power Play by Eve Gladstone

By day Annie and Peter were consultants who fought on opposite sides of the political fence. Peter still worked for the man who had shattered Annie's dreams, but that didn't prevent their after-hours battle for their hearts.

An Old-Fashioned Love by Amanda York

Gwen Halliday was a southern belle dressed in crinolines and Cade Landry was wearing a Union uniform when the Civil War was fought again. But when the game of make-believe was over it was clear that the love of the soldier for his southern lady was no fantasy.